Finding Love
In Distant Lands

Two Islands – Two Stories

Mary Mageau

Finding Love in Distant Lands

Copyright © 2010 by Mary Mageau

ISBN 978-1-4461-3289-0

Cover photograph by Mary Mageau

First published in 2010 by Lulu.com

'An Antique Brooch'

Hobart Town, Van Diemen's Land, 1852

Edith Rogers emerged from the sitting room, closed the door behind her and leaned back against it with a sigh of relief. Smiling she held her arms out to her daughters calling to them, 'Meg and Emily, everything is settled. Fanny is going to be married.'

'What wonderful news,' Meg replied. 'I'm so happy for Fanny.' Then she drew close to her mother.

'Just think, Fanny will soon be a bride.' Emily joined them both as she spoke.

'Now we must all move quietly away from the door as Fanny will see William out. They should be alone together at this time. And don't forget to choose a good dress for dinner tonight. It will be an important family affair.'

'Is something special happening tonight?' Emily asked.

'William will join us for dinner and afterward he and Father will meet in the library where he can formally request Father's permission to marry Fanny.'

'Why does he need Father's permission? We all know William and Fanny will marry anyway.' Emily countered.

'It's the way things are done today, Emily,' Meg replied, 'every marriage must be approved by the bride's father.'

That evening William Wakefield presented himself for dinner, carrying a bouquet of flowers for Edith. Everyone greeted him warmly then gathered around the table for a delicious meal. Their conversation was happy and animated. At the end of the dinner when the family rose to leave the dining room, William thanked Edith then turned nervously to Henry Rogers. The all important moment had finally arrived. 'May I speak privately with you, Sir?' William requested.

'Come into the library with me, William.' Then off they went together, closing the door behind them. The four women waited quietly in the drawing room. A short time later Henry opened the door and invited his wife and daughters to join them in the library.

'William has requested Fanny's hand in marriage and I have accepted his offer. He has a fine career ahead of him as a Solicitor-of-Law and I'm delighted to have a member of the legal fraternity join our family. I know you will love, cherish and care for my daughter, William, and I wish both you and Fanny a long and happy life together.'

'Thank you, Sir, for your permission. Although I am not a magistrate as you are, I have earned my qualifications and am now successfully practicing within the legal system. I love my beautiful Fanny and marrying her will make me the happiest man in all of Hobart Town.' And so it was settled and the evening finished with happy laughter and glasses of port raised in celebration.

Afterward the three sisters gathered in Fanny's bedroom. Excitedly Meg asked, 'Have you chosen a date for your wedding, Fanny?'

'We will celebrate an early April wedding in the Holy Trinity Church. We both chose Holy Trinity because the organ is new and it has such a lovely tone. And while we are talking about the wedding I want you, Meg, to join my best friend Anne, as a bridesmaid. Emily, will you be our flower girl?'

'Yes,' they answered excitedly. 'We would love to be part of the wedding party.'

Edith knocked lightly at Fanny's door then joined her daughters. All four of them crowded together on Fanny's bed as Edith spoke.

'There is so much to prepare before your April wedding. You and William will have to secure your date and organize for the banns to be read. A dressmaker will have to be hired to design and sew your gowns. There is a guest list to choose, invitations and flowers to order and refreshments to plan for your reception afterward. And with Christmas only a few months away, we have just half a year to get ready for this wonderful event.'

'Don't worry, Mother. All of us, together with Aunt Mary and Uncle Michael, will lend a hand.' Meg replied.

'This is all so exciting,' Emily added, 'that I can't wait until I get married too.'

'One at a time, please!' Mother laughed. 'Just think I'll have three brides to contend with and three weddings to plan with them. Never mind, I wouldn't exchange my darling daughters for all the money in the world.'

'I'm getting sleepy now.' Fifteen year old Emily yawned and stretched her arms above her head.

'Girls, look at the time. It's late so off to bed now, all of you. We can talk about the wedding tomorrow.'

A buzz of excitement carried them along for weeks. Then that fateful day arrived, when Father received an official letter that turned everything upside down.

2

One afternoon Henry arrived home early. 'How lovely to see you here so soon,' Edith greeted him with surprise, 'but you look tired. Are you feeling well?'

'Edith, can we speak alone in the library. I don't want the girls to be made aware of what I have to tell you.'

'I'll send for afternoon tea so we can have some refreshments as you share this news.'

Minutes later as they were seated Henry produced a letter. 'Yesterday I was contacted by the Home Secretary regarding his urgent need for a Stipendiary Magistrate to assist the Government of Van Diemen's Land. It seems that the penal settlement on Norfolk Island, which is under his jurisdiction, is slowly being closed down. Nearly half of the prisoners have already been relocated to Port Arthur. Many of the prisoners are violent men who have been subjected to years of cruelty by brutal commandants. It is necessary that this prison settlement now be closed.'

Edith reflected on his words. 'We have both heard rumours about the penitentiary and the shame that surrounds it. But how do these events affect you and why did you receive a letter?'

'At present there is no magistrate on Norfolk Island and a number of charges and misdemeanors still remain to be conducted through the usual court proceedings. Some fairly extensive paper-work and prison records will also have to be organized for removal to Port Arthur when the last prisoner departs.'

As Henry looked at Edith she dreaded hearing what else he would tell her. 'I have been ordered to accept this vacant position for a period of eleven months. I will sail right after Christmas and will return to Hobart Town in November of next year. By then the prisoners, most of the assigned military, and the civil administration will have left Norfolk.'

'Oh do you have to leave us so near the time of Fanny's wedding? Who will escort our daughter down the aisle and present her to William?'

'I have tried unsuccessfully to convince the Home Secretary to find a replacement but another magistrate cannot be found. As a member of the British Empire, I must fulfill my duty to England and to Queen Victoria. And didn't we always teach our daughters that fulfilling their duty is of primary importance?'

'Yes, we have always done so and I must stand strong and support you now.' Edith could hold her tears back no longer.

'I have to ask another sacrifice of you as well. I would be grateful if Meg would also accompany me. I will require her companionship and her ability to manage our home. I believe Norfolk Island has a very busy social life and Meg's skill as a hostess will often be called upon.'

'Meg is dreaming of the day when she will be Fanny's bridesmaid. She is so young, barely seventeen, yet Meg will be required to assume these adult responsibilities.'

'My dearest Edith, dry your eyes and let us finish this conversation for the present. Do not speak to the girls yet as I have a meeting tomorrow morning with Dr Robert Willson, the Catholic Prelate here in Hobart Town. He has made three visits to Norfolk Island over a number of years and he will have much to tell me about the situation there. After I've spoken to him, I'll call you and our daughters together and I'll break this distressing news. Meanwhile carry on bravely until tomorrow evening. I appreciate your support and strength so much, dearest Edith, during this difficult time.'

The following morning Henry arrived for his scheduled meeting with Bishop Willson. He was ushered into the Bishop's study. After being seated, Henry produced his letter from the Home Secretary and stated the reasons for his Norfolk appointment.

'Let me congratulate you, Your Honour, upon your selection. I am convinced you are the right magistrate to fulfill this duty. As you know I visited the Kings Town penal settlement on Norfolk Island during February and March of this year and found conditions unbearable for the prisoners. On my return to Hobart Town I sent a long report to England, strongly advising that the settlement be closed immediately.'

'Can you brief me on the conditions that led to your report, Your Grace?' Henry asked. 'I must know something of what to expect when I arrive.'

'The English Prison System, with its emphasis on prisoner isolation, has built a series of tiny, dark solitary confinement cells, all enclosed behind a high stone wall. Prisoners are worked to death, fed little if any nourishing food and punished for the slightest misdemeanour. Floggings are almost constant. When I offered a church service on Sunday 14th March, 270 men attended. Of these only 52 were without chains. The situation there is deplorable.'

'How many prisoners are still held on the island?' Henry asked.

'In 1845 there were about 1,400 prisoners living in dilapidated and inadequate buildings. Since my report of this year, large numbers of the worst offenders have been removed and relocated to Port Arthur, here in Van Diemen's Land. By the time you reach Norfolk Island there will be some 700 prisoners still serving their sentences, but these numbers should decrease quickly during 1853.'

'And what are the living conditions like for the civil and administrative officials, their wives and families?'

'There is a strong and reliable military contingent of marines from the 99th Brigade that guards the settlement. They are housed in large military barracks, close to the Commissariat Store, at the beginning of Quality Row. The houses for the government workers follow down the Row in a series of well landscaped, elegant first-and second-class homes. Many have five or six rooms, a walled courtyard and detached kitchen, with the staff quarters, bathhouse and laundry located in the annex, along the back wall. Kings Town residents also boast of their fine library, a small theatre, a meeting room and dwellings for the Catholic and Church of England priests. This aspect of the settlement has been well built by members of the Royal Architects and Engineers. The commandant's residence, Government House, is an elegant mansion in the Regency style, located on the top of a knoll, surrounded by magnificent pine trees. The atmosphere is pleasant and the social life is lively. The Stipendiary Magistrate's house is very grand, although I have not visited there nor seen its interior. You will be well housed and looked after during your stay.'

'I would like my seventeen year old daughter, Margaret, to accompany me. Will she find companions there to her liking?'

'There are several young women, wives and daughters of government officials, who will befriend her. She will not be lonely when you are away and will undoubtedly make new friends as she invites these various ladies to take afternoon tea with her. There are also sewing circles, reading groups and many of those parties of pleasure called picnics, into the surrounding areas of Cascade and Longridge Stations. All in all, her time spent with you should be safe and enjoyable.'

As Henry rose to thank Bishop Willson for the valuable information he provided, he left with a much lighter heart. 'Today I will speak to my family, as the time to do this is now upon me,' he thought. 'There will be many things to organize before Meg and I must pack and be away.'

Edith was eagerly awaiting his arrival and the two of them withdrew again into the library. Henry shared all that he had learned from Bishop Willson as Edith expressed her great sense of relief. 'Henry, you have brought me some peace of mind. I won't fret and worry so much now about the life you and Meg will experience on Norfolk Island.'

'If the girls are home at this moment, let's call them into the library, Edith, and I will finally share this news with them. The time is right to do so.'

'They are here so I'll summon them now.'

Fanny, Meg and Emily joined their parents as Henry showed them his letter, then spoke about what Bishop Willson told him of Norfolk Island. Shocked surprise was their first reaction, then the tears began to fall.

'Oh Father, you and Meg can't leave us at this time,' the girls chorused. 'Who will help us with the wedding?'

They asked many questions and Fanny was assured that her Uncle Michael had already been approached and would take on her father's role during the wedding.

'Meg, I haven't forgotten about you either.' Edith countered. I've set up a series of riding lessons, as you will be expected to ride horse-back on Norfolk Island.'

'Oh, Mother, you know I'm afraid of riding after I was thrown the last time I sat on a horse.'

'I've also planned three lessons for you with Miss Brown at her Academy of Decorum. You will be expected to act as Father's hostess and Miss Brown will prepare you well for these duties.'

Father concluded their meeting, 'I made every effort that I could to secure a replacement but none could be found. Mother and I have always taught you, our dear daughters, that the fulfillment of your duty is of prime importance. In this instance it will be difficult but I know each one of you will rise to this occasion. Be of good cheer as Meg and I will return before Christmas of next year.'

Over the following days the shock of Father's announcement was accepted. All their worries were slowly discussed, worked through and laid to rest.

3

Meg spent the next ten weeks musing and packing, preparing and worrying. Shortly after Father made his announcement Meg appeared at her sister's door. 'Fanny, can we talk in your bedroom?' They hugged each other as they sat close together on the bed. Meg began to cry then wiped her eyes as Fanny comforted her.

'You don't know how much I will suffer being away from you, Mother and Emily. And now I'll also miss your wedding! Why do I have to leave home for a year to be in that awful place on Norfolk Island?'

'Meg, Father needs you to keep him company and maintain the running of his home. Think of the new people you will meet, the places you will see. The year will fly by and you'll both be home again in no time.'

They spoke on and on, as Fanny's words eased Meg's fears. 'What would I do without you, my dearest Fanny. You've always been a good friend to me as well as a sister.'

Meg's first obstacle was overcome when she conquered her fear of mounting a horse and directing it while riding side-saddle. After several weeks she could enjoy a canter with complete confidence. However, her attendance at Miss Brown's Academy was another story altogether.

Meg rang the bell outside an imposing sandstone building with the sign, *Academy of Decorum*, displayed above the door. A housemaid invited her into a sitting room where a woman, clad in a voluminous brown dress, nodded for her to be seated.

'Miss Brown, I am Meg Rogers. Thank you for accepting me into your academy.'

'Young lady, here you will not be called "Meg." You are Mistress Margaret Rogers and thus shall I address you.'

'Yes, Miss Brown.'

'Look at your posture, slumped back into the chair with your feet apart! Sit up forward in the chair with your back straight. Place your arms at your sides with your hands resting together in your lap. Never spread your feet apart. The legs must remain close together with your right foot slightly crossed over the left.'

'Is this better now?' Meg asked tentatively.

'You must endeavour to sit in this way at all times. Now you appear demure and contained, as a young lady should. Look behind you at the wall. What do you see there?'

'I see a portrait of Queen Victoria.'

'Notice how she sits. Our Queen is the perfect example for a young woman to emulate. Always think of her, for here in my academy Queen Victoria will also be watching you.' Meg's back began to ache and she longed to relax for a moment but under Miss Brown's beady eyes this was not to be.

Miss Brown was a large woman, with folds of flesh that hung loosely below her cheeks. When she moved her head her jowls shook menacingly. She wore a small yellow shawl over her neck and shoulders and a red knitted cap covered her hair. In her brown dress she reminded Meg of an oversized scrub turkey. Oh, if only this lesson would come to an end.

'Next to you on the small table lies a folio filled with papers. They are yours to keep. Take them up and look through them now.'

Meg noted several replies to various forms of invitation, as well as sample letters inviting persons to afternoon tea and dinner.

'You and your father will receive many invitations to social gatherings. I have visited Norfolk Island myself and I have prepared several young women to encounter its social life. Whenever an invitation arrives this must be acknowledged, whether you choose to attend it or not. Your reply must be sent back on the second or third day, never any later. A written response on fine white paper is the acceptable means of doing so. The same applies to invitations you wish to issue. Have you any questions thus far?'

'No Miss Brown. These samples will be very helpful to me.'

'There is also a journal beneath these sample papers. You must keep track of every invitation you receive together with the name of the person who sent it and the date of its reception. And you should date the reply that you send your response back to the sender.'

'Thank you for this information, Miss Brown. I appreciate your providing these samples for my use.'

'When you begin to meet people try to memorize their names. Always seek to learn where they rank within the social system; the size and style of house they inhabit will assist you. It is our English way, that everyone must know their place. Take the papers and journal away with you now and when you arrive tomorrow, I want to see one of your hand copied replies to an afternoon tea, as well as an invitation from you to a guest, to attend a dinner. Use the sample papers as a format. Tomorrow I will teach you the proper way to preside at the tea table and later, at the dinner table.'

'Thank you, Miss Brown. This has all been very helpful and I will return tomorrow.' Then as quickly as she could, Meg escaped outside into the sunshine.

Tomorrow arrived all too soon as Meg set out again for the dreaded Academy of Decorum. There she awaited Miss Brown, sitting stiffly as a proper young lady should. When Miss Brown was seated Meg offered the samples of her hand written invitation, together with her response. Nervously she held her breath as Miss Brown read them.

'Mistress Margaret Rogers, you have a beautiful, flowing style of penmanship. Do you write often?'

'Yes, Miss Brown. I keep journals filled with my own poetry and stories.' Meg breathed a sigh of relief.

'Writing is a fine activity. Always remember that an idle mind is the devil's workshop! Keep on with your writing. '

'I intend to do so, Miss Brown.'

'Come with me now to the tea table as you will preside over many tea parties with the women of Norfolk Island. I will sit here, on your left, and you will occupy the empty chair next to me.'

Meg noted her beautifully laid table, dressed in fine linen and set with an exquisite china tea set. They sat down together as a housemaid carried in a pot of steaming tea.

'Always have the tea pot placed slightly forward on your right. The visitor with the highest rank should occupy your immediate left with the others seated as benefits their station. When rank is not an issue the eldest woman is usually served first with the younger ones following. Reach out your left hand and she will offer her cup and saucer. Place them on the table, pick up the tea pot in your right hand with your left hand resting on the lid. Then carefully fill her cup, just above the halfway mark. Put the pot down, pick up her cup and offer it back to her. Never pour the tea too quickly or it will spill into the saucer. Now, pour the tea for me, please.'

Meg was trembling as she reached out her hand to accept Miss Brown's cup and saucer. She couldn't control her shaking hand and the tea spoon fell out of the saucer onto the table. She felt Miss Brown's eyes boring into her.

'Excuse me, Miss Brown. I've dropped the spoon. '

'Pick it up by its handle and replace the spoon. Now please pour my tea.'

Meg was so uncomfortable the tea pot shook, spilling tea all over the saucer.

'I've made another mistake, Miss Brown. Will I ever get this right?'

'You will persevere at home, and with practice you will perfect the etiquette of the tea table. Practice, practice; as this must be done well if you wish to be accepted socially.'

Her final appointment with Miss Brown included a lesson on how to preside successfully at the dinner table. 'Fashion dictates that many courses are usually served. You must give the signal to a staff member when every guest has finished their course. The waitress will clear and remove the empty plates and silver.

Always wait for a brief time before signaling the arrival of the next course. 'Do you understand?'

'Yes Miss Brown.'

Miss Brown continued. 'It is most likely that on Norfolk Island you will serve only an entrée, a main course and a dessert. I can recall a formal dinner I attended here in Hobart Town, where six courses were served. Norfolk will not be so grand, but you must still strive to be the perfect hostess.'

Before she could finally leave the academy, Miss Brown discussed her wardrobe and its requirements. 'Kings Town is often windy and thankfully you have a sensible hair style. It is wise to part your hair down the centre, comb it back behind your head and secure it into a bun. You will need two bonnets; shawls both light and knitted for colder days. There are few opportunities to buy fabric and make clothing so be sure to pack all that you will need, together with a riding habit and hat. Unlike the French with all their silly fripperies, fine food and fancy dress, we English wear good sensible shoes and clothing.' Then Miss Brown leaned forward and raised her voice as her jowls shook. 'I have even heard that the women of France who accompany their husbands to Tahiti, all bring their dressmakers with them. Just imagine, always being presented in the height of fashion, to move among natives and savages!'

At last her ordeal was over and Meg could finally leave. 'Thank you, Miss Brown, for all the assistance you have given me. I feel more confident now to take on the role of a social hostess, for Father and myself.'

4

Meg and her father set sail aboard HMS *Fortitude*. After a remarkably smooth voyage, on the nineteenth day a welcome cry was heard from the ship's captain. 'Land Ho! Norfolk Island lies ahead, off the forward bow.' Everyone rushed to the fore deck where a tiny speck of green could barely be seen in the vast ocean of rolling waves. 'We should be reaching Kings Town early on the day after tomorrow.'

'At last we can leave this ship and stand on firm land again.' Meg squeezed her father's arm.

'Yes, Meg, it will be such a joy to leave this dark, cramped ship for our own home.'

An island surrounded by steep cliffs slowly came into view. As their ship drew near the shore, a small strip of beach was sighted. It was surrounded by two beautiful bays, with Kings Town stretching far along on the hillside above. Lines of homes and other buildings appeared spacious and comfortable, even from this distance. On the beach Meg could make out a gray fortress of solid stone forming a high quadrangle.

'Meg, the enclosed stone building you are pointing out to me houses the prisoners. When we have settled and you decide to go walking, never venture down to the beach near this place. There will be many other safe spaces for you to visit and explore, up in the hills and away from here,' Father spoke firmly.

As a reef enclosed the beach, protecting it from the swells of the sea, their ship dropped anchor a distance from the shore. Meg watched as a long boat, with four oarsmen, made its way toward them. The captain approached Meg and her father.

'Your Honour, you and your daughter, Mistress Margaret will be the first passengers to depart our ship. We will assist you and your luggage into the long boat. On the pier, Captain Rupert Deering, commandant of the penal settlement is waiting to greet you. '

Meg and Henry successfully descended a small ladder into the boat and were seated as their sea chests were lowered carefully. Soon they drew up next to the pier, and stepped at last onto the shores of Norfolk Island.

'Welcome, Your Honour and Mistress Margaret. I am Captain Rupert Deering, Penal Administrator for the 99th Regiment, The Lanarks. We are all so happy that you both arrived safely.'

Henry and Meg acknowledged the greeting, breathing a sigh of relief that they had landed at last. In no time they were able to walk comfortably on land again.

'I have four marines at the ready, loading your belongings on a horse cart to take you to your residence. I've also instructed them to make a short tour of our settlement along the way. You and I will be working closely together, Sir. And Mistress Margaret, please feel free to call on me if my services are ever needed. It is our hope that you both will enjoy your time spent here.'

One by one the men lifted their boxes and luggage aboard the cart. First Meg sighted her travel trunk with all her personal effects and Father's larger trunk with his books, papers and personal effects. A small wooden box marked, **Handle With Care**, contained her farewell gift from Edith. Meg knew it included a fine china tea set with a large tea pot, cream jug and sugar bowl, six plates, saucers and cups. Linen table cloths and matching napkins completed its contents. These would be used for her social gatherings at home. 'Meg, you may need this on Norfolk Island and after you and Father return it will be yours to keep. Every time you use it, think of us back at home.' Edith, Fanny and Emily all presented the gift on her last day and helped to pack it. Meg was pleased to notice how gently the men handled her precious cargo.

The final item, a small crate, carried her davenport, made from timber with a matching chair. 'You will have free time to devote to your writing on the island and I thought your own little desk would be a fine piece of furniture for you to use,' Henry suggested. 'It's important to have something of your own close by and who knows, you may even return with a finished book or a collection of short poetry.'

Off they went, past the Royal Engineers Office, the Police Station, the convict store and hospital, up Pier Street toward the elegant buildings of Quality Row. Their young soldier driver, first pointed out the four storey Commissariat Store, secured behind a high stone wall.

'This is the life line of the settlement,' he told them. 'Every time a ship reaches us it is filled with supplies and mail as well as passengers. Everyone comes to the Commissariat Store to order their food supplies and goods. We stock all items that we are not able to grow or to make ourselves.'

'I see a large herd of cattle grazing on the hills behind Quality Row.' Father enquired, 'Do you butcher your own beef supply here?'

'Yes, one of our free settlers is a butcher. He also operates a poultry farm so we always have chickens and fresh eggs available. Delicious fish are abundant in these waters and can be caught easily. Potatoes, corn, onions, pumpkins, beans and silver beet are cultivated at Longridge Station and brought to the store. Apples, paw paw and bananas also grow. Here on Norfolk Island we eat very well.'

'What is that next large building and the other nearby resembling the first one?' Meg asked.

'They are the Old and New Military Barracks, set close by the officers' bath house and the Parade Grounds. It was deemed important to build the Commissariat Store near the barracks, for the protection our food supplies.'

One after another stately home was passed on Quality Row. Tall pine trees and smaller shrubs added to its sense of peaceful order. Father enquired of the driver, 'All the buildings are constructed from stone. Do you have an operational quarry nearby?'

'Yes, here in Kings Town and over at Emily Bay coral rock can be quarried and worked into blocks by the convicts. But now that this settlement is being evacuated, there is no need to operate the quarry any longer.'

Meg noticed that the houses had different size frontages. 'Why do some homes appear to be built on larger allotments than others?'

'All first class houses have frontages of fifty-one feet, second class homes are allowed forty-six feet and the third class quarters are built on thirty foot allotments. The Stipendiary Magistrate's residence is a first class house.'

Another young soldier called out, 'Stop the horses for a minute and look down the road we are passing on the right. Through the trees is our Government House, built in the Georgian style, on the top of Dove Hill. It's a magnificent mansion and its position is in keeping with the social supremacy of our British Military system. Here the Commandant is able to overlook all the elements of the Kings Town settlement from his front veranda. By designing Kings Town in this way, every person will know his place within the system.'

'I am amazed at the structure and order of this colony.' Father replied. 'It will be a pleasure to complete my work here.'

At last the horse cart drew up before an elegant home, at the far end of Quality Row. The frontage of the house had been reversed to face away from the Row so that its southerly aspect provided the occupants with a pleasant view of tall spruce pines. It was also better shielded from the strong winds and storms that occasionally blew in from the sea. Meg and her father moved across the front garden where they were greeted at the front door.

'Welcome to you both, Your Honour and your daughter, Mistress Margaret. I'm Annie, your housekeeper, and I hope you will find everything here to your liking.' She proceeded to show them through the house. A large sitting room, a small library and the dining room were entered on the right off a long corridor. On the left of this hallway was a large bedroom with a double window that looked out towards the sea. Next to it was a smaller bedroom and an adjoining study. The home was clean and comfortably furnished.

'Meg, I'd like you to settle into the large bedroom. I will claim the smaller one, as the study will serve as my home office. I'll be spending time away from the house and you should have a large space for your desk where you can relax, read and write. I'll ask the soldiers to bring in our travel chests and they can assist us with unpacking your little desk and chair. The tea set can be placed in the dining room for the present.'

After everything was brought into the house and the horse cart departed Annie approached them. 'You must both be feeling very hungry and it's nearly lunch time. If you would like to come into the dining room I'll have a light meal ready for you. But first, let me show you the back garden so that you can inspect the annex. '

Meg and her father followed Annie into an enclosed courtyard that contained a table, two chairs, and several large fruit trees – paw paw, banana and mandarin. The annex across the back wall included Annie's bedroom, the kitchen, a bath house and privy. A cottage garden filled with herbs and flowers lay outside her kitchen door. 'Take a minute to refresh yourselves then I'll serve your lunch.'

Later Meg and Father were seated in the dining room where Annie carried in bowls of vegetable beef soup, warm scones, soft cottage cheese and a jug of cool water. As they enjoyed the first meal in their new home, both agreed that their stay on Norfolk Island was off to a fine beginning. Father squeezed her hand as he spoke. 'My mind is now at rest, Meg. Thank you for agreeing to accompany me as I know how difficult it was for you to leave Hobart Town. Norfolk Island will be happy and fulfilling.' Meg returned an affectionate squeeze. 'Yes it will, Father, and I am happy to be here. Norfolk Island will provide a wonderful experience for us both.'

5

The following morning, as Father and Meg finished their breakfast, Captain Deering arrived. 'Come in and join us for a cup of tea.' Annie brought a cup and saucer and Meg filled his cup. 'I won't be dropping spoons and spilling tea any more,' she thought. 'I'm confident away from Miss Brown. In fact I enjoy being a hostess.'

'After you finish here Sir, would you please make your way to the Old Military Barracks? We have set up a court room where your litigations will be conducted. There is also an adjoining study that you could use for an office and meeting room. A volume of paper work has been stored here for you to peruse and pack, and this will be shipped back to Port Arthur. If you wish I can make a soldier available on a part-time basis, to act as your clerk.'

'I'm looking forward to beginning this phase of my work,' Father replied. 'I understand from the Home Office that there will be quite a back log of paper work to organize.'

'The *Fortitude* that brought you here will be sailing in three more days. You have two convicts to sentence for theft and assault charges. These men and twenty-nine other prisoners will be transported when the ship departs.'

Captain Deering turned to Meg. 'If you have any mail to send back to Van Diemen's Land, please bring it to the Commissariat Store. Our chief clerk, Mr Stewart, will attend to all your letters and parcels. Be sure to take a look around the store as each ship brings in new items. I know that you ladies are always interested in knitting wool, sewing notions and fabric. Occasionally we even sell blouses, shawls and collars. There is also a library and meeting room behind the store, used by the free settlers. It's a good place where one can read quietly or borrow books to take home.'

'I'm looking forward to exploring Quality Row,' Meg replied, 'and it will be so easy, as everything is within a comfortable walking distance.'

After Father left for his working morning Meg returned to her bedroom. She had finished most of their personal unpacking and set up the wardrobe and chest of drawers in each room. Moving to her desk she spread out her own writing materials, the folio and journal from Miss Brown, her pencils, ink and pens. Her much loved Toby jug had survived the voyage and he would be filled with writing implements. She found her stationery, then began the joyful task of writing her first letter to Mother, Fanny and Emily. There was so much to tell them about the voyage and their arrival in Kings Town. By lunch she had filled four sheets and signed off with love from herself and Father. The envelope was addressed, sealed and put aside until she would visit the store in the afternoon.

'Father, you are home already and I'm suddenly feeling hungry. It's already time for lunch and I don't know where the morning went.' They made their way to the dining room where Annie brought in bread, cheese and soup.

'I will be conducting my first court this afternoon, Meg, to sentence two prisoners for transportation. Afterward, I will work in my office until late afternoon, then I'll return home. This may be the pattern that many of my days will take.'

'After lunch I will take the letter I wrote this morning to the Commissariat Store and look around,' Meg replied. 'When I come back I'll rest and do some reading. Maybe I'll even meet some of the settlers along the way today.'

Meg started off along the wide roadway, admiring the beautiful homes as she passed each gate. Two of the twelve houses looked as though they were empty. 'I suppose some families are packing up and moving to Port Arthur already,' she thought. At another large home near the Commissariat Store, several women had gathered on the veranda, busy with their needlework. As Meg passed by they waved to her, smiled and called out a greeting.

Meg entered the store and gave her letter to the Commissariat clerk, who pasted postage stamps on the envelope. 'Ah, you must be Mistress Margaret Rogers, daughter of the new Stipendiary Magistrate.'

'Yes, I am. Father and I arrived yesterday and he is already at work while I settle us in.' Meg paid for the stamps, as she scanned the large interior of the store.

'I'll make sure that your letter reaches the departing ship as your family back home will want to know if you arrived safely. And take a look around as I still have quite a few goods in stock. '

Meg's eyes fell upon a counter filled with items that a home maker would enjoy. Several glass vases were on display with china plates of all sizes, cup and saucer settings and silver serving utensils. Small gifts in the form of dainty drawstring bags, baskets and table linens filled the lower shelf. Large cast iron cooking pots with lids were placed on the floor along the front. As she gazed at these items a voice behind her called out, 'Welcome. '

Meg turned to face a young woman, just a little older than herself, smiling as she extended her hands. 'You must be Mistress Margaret Rogers and I've been waiting for you to arrive here.'

'Yes, I am she, but please just call me Meg. And who are you?'

'My name is Elizabeth Lockwood, but everyone calls me Beth. I live with my mother and father at Number 8. He is the Commissariat Officer for the settlement. Several families with children have left us for Port Arthur and I've been hoping that another young woman would arrive. It's been rather lonely here these last few months.'

'I'm pleased that we found one another so soon and I look forward to your company, Beth.'

'Come over to the sewing goods with me as I must buy some knitting wool. I want to begin work on a scarf for my father, and you can help me choose the colour.'

The young women moved toward two counters in a corner. The first contained several shawls and large bolts of printed cloth, suitable for a woman's skirt or jacket. Three white cotton blouses hung from hangers on hooks and samples of lace, sewing cotton and knitting yarns were spread over the second counter.

'What colour yarn would you choose for a man's scarf, Meg?'

'I like the light brown tweed wool with the little fleck in it,' Meg replied.

'That is the one I also like. I'll buy two skeins now and when I get home I'll start to knit right away.'

Beth paid for her purchase and the two moved outside. Meg asked her, 'Are you able to come to my home tomorrow for morning tea? I live at Number 1, the last house on Quality Row.'

'Thank you, Meg. I will be there. We can talk and get to know one another better.'

Meg returned home with a sense of joy. Already she had found a friend, someone of her own age, someone that she could spend time with. 'I must show Beth the story that I'm writing,' Meg thought. 'I think she will enjoy hearing about, *Toby's Travels*. She may even teach me how to knit, as I've always wanted to learn this skill.'

Beth reached her home and excitedly told her mother about Meg, the new friend she had just met. 'Mother I hope Meg and I can take walks together on Sunday afternoons. You won't let me walk alone but if there are two of us, and we stay close to the settlement, you wouldn't mind, would you?'

'Not at all. I'm so pleased you found someone to spend time with as I know how lonely you've been lately.'

'And tomorrow I've been invited to morning tea at Meg's home, Mother.'

'Be sure to go along and take a little gift with you.'

'I have just the thing for her, a lace bookmark I hand knit some time ago. I think that she will like it.'

And so began a fine friendship that would last far after Beth left Kings Town.

6

Several days later Father returned from work with exciting news. 'Meg, one of my duties here is to inspect all facilities in the penal settlement, then send a report back to Hobart Town. A brig will be arriving in three weeks, to transport another group of convicts to Port Arthur. Among them are two prisoners, presently working at the Longridge Station. I must interview them both, as outstanding charges laid against them should be prosecuted. Would you like to join me for a few days at Longridge?'

'I was hoping we might visit the farm there. Beth told me that the agricultural superintendant's house and gardens are very attractive,' she replied excitedly.

'We will leave tomorrow morning and ride the mile and a half on horseback. Captain Deering and another marine will act as our escort. You can pack a little case with your change of clothing, books or anything else you would need. One of the soldiers will travel in a small horse cart where our boxes will be carried.'

'How long will we be away, Father?'

'Plan to be away for two full days and one overnight. Would you also ask Annie to pack a light lunch and some water, enough for four travelers? Along the way we will stop for a rest. There is a spot where a table and benches have been set up under a great tree. It's frequently used for picnics by groups of settlers.'

'I'll have some free time to work on my stories for, *Toby's Travels*. I can hardly wait to see the farm!'

Meg went to the kitchen to let Annie know that they would be away for two days. She was delighted to have some time free for herself and assured Meg that a mid-morning lunch would be ready for them the following day. Then Meg did some packing and laid out her riding habit and hat. She would see more of the island tomorrow and its unique scenery. The tall pines seemed to grow everywhere and in even the slightest wind, they filled the land with their murmuring sounds. The Norfolk scenery was so beautiful.

After breakfast a marine leading two extra horses arrived at the gate. As he packed their belongings in a small cart, Father assisted Meg to mount her horse, a gentle little mare named, Lady. 'I'm pleased he was able to find a side-saddle for me,' Meg thought. Father swung onto his large grey stallion and they were off. Led by Captain Deering, their party passed all the homes on Quality Row, the barracks and Commissariat Store, to move west toward the Longridge Station.

A narrow dirt road twisted through native forest so they travelled slowly. After an hour in the saddle the picnic spot was reached, and Meg was happy to dismount and stretch her legs. She set about unpacking their lunch, spreading out a cloth and setting a large plate on the table. It was filled with buttered bread and thick slices of roast beef. The repast finished with fresh apples and a flask of water. Everyone's energy was restored and their journey continued.

The native bush slowly gave way to large cultivated fields. A number of them also lay fallow. Captain Deering gave them his account of the Longridge Station. 'When the settlement was at full strength there were five hundred convicts working here, supervised by sixty soldiers. Corn, rye, barley, oats and peas were all cultivated. As you can see only a few large fields are still planted yet our harvest has been more that enough to feed the entire colony. By the end of next year, all of this will have closed down.'

'Do those wooden barracks house the present workers and military?' Father asked.

'They do, and if you look ahead behind this stand of trees, you will see the homestead.'

Meg replied, 'It's such a large and elegant house!'

'Of particular interest are the domestic gardens where a number of flowers native to England have been transplanted. Mr Gilbert Robertson, our previous Agricultural Superintendent, lived here with his wife and four daughters until he resigned in 1847. One of his daughters, Elizabeth, died here and is buried in the Kings Town cemetery.'

As they reached the house James, an old marine and his wife, Flo came out to greet them. In no time all were settled, Father was away with Captain Deering and Meg found herself alone. After a change of clothing and a brief rest she went in search of Flo.

'Is there a place where I might spread out my writing? I'd like to do some quiet work.'

'I would offer you the dining room table but I believe this room will be used as a temporary courthouse this afternoon. If you walk to the centre of the garden you will see a lovely little summer house, with a table and chair inside. You could use this any time you wish, Mistress Meg.'

Meg gathered her materials, took up her shawl and found the summer house. The porch was covered with a passion fruit plant and several pieces of fruit were ripening on the vine. Inside she settled herself at the table. 'This is perfect,' she thought. 'Here I can work in peace on completing another of *Toby's Travels.*' But before beginning, Meg took a few moments to recall how this project had started.

Back in Hobart Town, she and Fanny often visited the shops in the business district. Among them was a book store owned by a writer, Mr Fossett, who operated a small printing press and bindery behind his shop. Together with a friend he published a selection of books on the history of local places, and a few novels. Meg noticed however, that there were no available books or stories suitable for children. Since Mr. Fossett had already read some of her poetry, Meg discussed the idea for *Toby's Travels*, a collection of short stories featuring the adventures of an itinerant Toby jug. Mr. Fossett was interested and suggested that she prepare a manuscript to submit on her return. So here she was, hard at work now on her first large writing project.

When Meg was twelve years old her aunt and uncle sent her a Royal Doulton Toby jug from London. He was a squat little figure dressed in a long coat with a cravat, knee breeches and buckled shoes. His tricorn hat formed a pouring spout and a handle was attached to his back.

'Why is he called, Toby?' Meg asked.

'It's possible he has been named after Sir Toby Belch, a character in Shakespeare's Twelfth Night,' Father replied.

In her first story, Toby has been found missing as Kate, his owner, prepares to leave the ship she has been travelling on. She has searched for Toby without finding a single clue as to where he might be. As Kate walks sadly toward the gangplank to disembark, she hears a familiar laugh.

Looking up Kate discovers Toby. He is standing high above her head, on the yard-arm. 'Toby, you naughty jug, come down at once!' He only laughs again. 'Jump down and I'll catch you.' Instead Toby turns around, with his back toward Kate and gazes longingly out to sea.

'Well then, you stay here and continue your travels. But when I get home, I'm going to buy a new jug to take your place. At last I'll have a Toby who won't be a run- away.

Kate awoke the next morning in her own warm bed. It was a wonderful journey she thought, until her eyes fell upon the empty place where Toby used to stand. She sat up in bed with a start. Toby was right in the spot where he usually stood. Crossing the room she took him in her arms and cried for joy, 'Toby, you've come back. Now you must be a good jug and always stay home where you belong.'

It was late afternoon when Meg made her way back to the big house to prepare for dinner. The delicious roast meal, prepared by the capable Flo, was accompanied by red wine. Afterward Father, Captain Deering, who everyone now called Rupert, and the escort marine invited Meg to join them for a game of whist. The card playing was so enjoyable they finished three rubbers before Meg finally excused herself and prepared for bed. During the following morning Father completed his work and after lunch all four found themselves riding back to Kings Town. Their visit to Longridge Station had passed all too quickly.

7

March was an exciting month. A piece of welcome news reached Meg when a ship was finally sighted approaching Kings Town.

'After the brig drops anchor and the long boats move cargo ashore, everyone visits the Commissariat Store on the following day to pick up their mail. By now you should have letters from home,' Annie explained.

'Father, tomorrow I'll walk to the store to collect our mail. I will also be meeting Beth who will help me select yarn and needles. She has offered to teach me how to knit.'

'We should have our first letters from home now. And what a good idea to take up a new craft, Meg. Knitting is a fine way to fill your time while making something useful to wear.'

Filled with anticipation Meg set off the next morning to discover five letters waiting – two for herself and three for Father. 'I'll wait until I get home so we can read them together,' Meg thought. Beth had also arrived to collect the letter waiting for her. The two friends made their way to the notions counter where Mr Stewart was adding more coloured yarns to the display case. He greeted the girls.

'Best to select all you need today as this is the last shipment of notions that will be coming in. Two more families are leaving us when the brig departs, so I'm starting to sell off as much of my stock as I can. The only other orders I will place now are for essential food supplies, gunpowder and bullets.'

'Meg, may I suggest two pairs of knitting needles of different lengths and thickness. I'd like you to knit a simple wash cloth for your first project. Then we will move on to a scarf that you could knit in several different colours. Purchase at least six different skeins of yarn today so we can begin this afternoon.'

'I'll knit the cloth for Annie from this cream colour. As the scarf will be for Father, please help me choose three yarns that would go well together and would suit a man's scarf.'

The knitting lesson began after lunch in the leafy courtyard of Beth's house. Meg struggled to cast on a small piece for her swatch. When this row was completed she practiced her garter stitch, the most basic of knitting stitches. 'I'm so slow and clumsy,' Meg thought, as she surveyed her first row of uneven stitches.

'You are doing well for a beginner, Meg. Don't become discouraged.'

'I'm not sure where the new stitch is, as I can't always see it. When I try to slip it on the right needle I sometimes drop it.'

'Watch me knit as I say the little rhyme that we all learn when we start. It goes like this –

"In through the front door, once around the back.

Peek through the window and off jumps Jack."

'Now I'll hold your hands in mine and we'll try it together again.' Beth guided Meg's hands and in no time she was knitting confidently on her own. Meg had also purchased a container to hold her needles and yarn and as she made her way home with the letters for herself and Father, she was eager to keep working on her new craft. 'One day I'll have a surprise for Father to wear in the cooler months,' she thought. 'This will please him so much.'

When Father returned home he and Meg went into the library to open their letters from Hobart Town. Meg read her letter from Mother first and realized how much she missed her family in Hobart Town. It wasn't easy to hide her tears as Edith included so many interesting items about the preparations for Fanny's wedding. Her letter finished with the following:

'We know how happy you are making your father, by looking after him and providing comfort and companionship. Do write my dearest Meg, with news of your life on Norfolk Island. We all miss you so much.'

Fanny and Emily had sealed their letters in the same envelope that included sketches of Fanny's wedding gown, her veil and the dress that Emily would be wearing. Everyone sounded so happy and Meg was relieved by their good news. Father, too, was delighted with all they had told him.

As the weeks passed, Meg and her father received dinner invitations drawing them into the social life of Kings Town. Rose, the wife of the Foreman of Works, hosted a Wednesday afternoon sewing circle on her large front veranda, followed by an afternoon tea. Beth brought Meg along with her, and she was made to feel welcome. Knitting and crocheting projects were shared, along with stories and friendly gossip. Meg reciprocated with a morning tea for the women and Annie baked beautiful scones served with jam and cream. Rupert regularly joined Meg and Father for Sunday lunch. The men either enjoyed card games afterward, or Meg read aloud to them from a novel. There were interesting books available from the library.

'The only thing missing now is a good chess partner,' Father told Meg.

'You know I play so poorly it's never a challenge for you, Father. You always win. Doesn't Rupert play chess?'

'No, he doesn't enjoy the game. But never fear as we have many social interests to keep us amused during our weekends.'

On the following Saturday afternoon Beth and Meg walked through the Kings Town cemetery to see if they could find Elizabeth Robertson's grave site. 'Just imagine, she was only twenty four years old in 1847 when she died from tuberculosis at Longridge Station. Poor Elizabeth is the only member of her family to be buried here on Norfolk.' Beth discovered some late blooming flowers in the adjoining woodland and the girls placed a small bouquet on Elizabeth's grave, which they located in the centre of a row. As the golden afternoon sun began set, they decided to walk to the shore of Emily Bay for a last view of the entire settlement before returning home.

Suddenly the prison foreshore exploded into a frenzy of activity. As three soldiers stood guard around a whaling boat, six convicts suddenly broke away and ran toward the boat. The three soldiers joined them as they stole the boat, pushed it into the water and tried to scramble inside. Loud yelling alerted all the marines and a dozen armed men ran down from the barracks on the hill behind. As the third soldier attempted to climb into the boat he lost his footing, then was captured and held. The stolen boat moved away quickly as the escapees rowed frantically, manning the six oars. Sounds of gunfire filled the air but the boat remained just out of reach of the hail of bullets. By the time a second boat, filled with armed marines was launched, darkness had begun to fall. With regret the pursuit was abandoned. Meanwhile the frightened girls quickly returned to their homes to convey the news.

Meg met Father at the front gate, as he was starting to run toward the prison area. 'Go inside, Meg and secure the front door. I'll call out to you and Annie when I return.'

'Take care, Father. Other prisoners may make a similar attempt or cause serious trouble.'

Meg told Annie what she and Beth had witnessed first hand. Her heart was pounding and only after Father returned an hour later, could she relax again.

'Tomorrow morning a larger boat will put out to sea to try to overtake the escapees. I don't like their chances though, as the prisoners and soldiers will row furiously all night,' Father remarked. Next morning luck favoured the escapees, as a heavy mist hung over the water and lifted late in the day. By then, only a tiny speck far out on the horizon could be sighted. The departing boat was now well beyond any range of pursuit.

'Rupert has already sent a message to the military and police on Van Diemen's Land. If the escapees have the good fortune to survive on the open sea in that small boat, they will be picked up. It was a desperate and foolish bid for freedom and who knows if they will arrive on dry land. Nothing but open sea lies between them and the mainland.'

'I feel sorry for the soldier who was captured and detained. I wouldn't want to be in his shoes right now,' Meg remarked. After this bold attempt at escape, the prison was secured and life settled into its daily routine once again.

8

'Meg, I realize this request is at short notice, but I have been asked to visit Cascade on the other side of the island. Would you like to accompany me?'

'Oh yes, I have wanted for some time to see Cascade Bay and visit the waterfall. And this trip will provide me with another adventure for Toby to take.'

'Can you be ready to leave tomorrow after lunch? Rupert will travel with us together with a small military escort. We won't ride on horseback, as Cascade lies directly north on the other side of the island. The trip takes several hours so you and I will ride in a large horse cart. If all goes well we will arrive at the Old Government Garden site to spend the next two nights there. The gardener and one domestic have rooms ready in a wooden cottage, but I warn you - it will be quite rustic. '

'Father, I'm always ready for any occasion and will pack some warm clothing. I'll travel again in my riding habit.'

Meg packed carefully before bed after alerting Annie that they would be away for a few days. The following morning she told Beth she would not see her for their usual Wednesday afternoon walk but would be in touch again for her Saturday knitting lesson. After an early lunch their escort arrived and packed the cart as Annie waved farewell from the front gate. The April day was sunny with a slight hint of autumn coolness. Rupert rode ahead while Father took the reins of the horse team. The two mounted soldiers followed. As they set off Meg learned interesting facts about the Cascade settlement.

'There are only two sites on this entire island suitable for bringing ships close to shore. These lie at Sydney Bay in Kings Town and Cascade Harbour. In 1792 convicts laboured to break up and remove several large rocks along the beach front, blocking the entrance to Cascade. When the area was cleared they constructed a jetty and installed a crane at its deep water edge. The place name is derived from a cascade that spills over a series of low falls, then plunges over a wall of black rock, to fall into the sea. Cascade Harbour still serves as a watering place for many ships and can be pressed into use when bad weather or strong winds make landing at Sydney Bay impossible.'

'Beth told me that the surrounding pine forests at Cascade are magnificent. She and her family visited some time ago and remarked on its strange and wild sort of beauty,' Meg replied.

'Rupert is serving as our escort because he is also a Justice of the Peace and can act as my notary. I need his legal services in cases pertaining to prisoners who will be transported.'

'Are there many prisoners serving on the Cascade farm?'

'I believe there are only ten prisoners working now with two marines acting as guards. Seven of them are being transported to Port Arthur and three have completed their sentences and are eligible for a pardon. This is one aspect of my work that I enjoy, that of informing men that they are free at last. Many of them are quite elderly and can decide to go ashore at Hobart

Town or continue on to Port Arthur, to take up paid work of their choosing.'

'What happens to the men who stop at Hobart Town? They have no families or friends to meet them. Where can they go to look for work or find food and shelter?'

'Several of the churches have houses set aside to care for them and offer help. Do you remember my speaking about the Catholic Prelate of Van Diemen's Land, Dr Robert Willson?'

'Yes, you had a meeting with him before we left and he was very helpful, Father.'

'Bishop Willson has created an exceptional programme to assist these former prisoners. It has proven so successful that governments and other churches have adopted its basic ideas to their own work in this field. Nothing makes me happier than to free a man who has suffered for so many years as these poor wretches have.'

'Father, you visited the prison and saw first hand what the life of a prisoner is like. Can you tell me about their treatment?'

'Meg, I hesitate as I'd like to shield you from these unpleasant facts.'

'Father, I want to know. I may even write about this one day and can't be sheltered forever. When I'm older and I have developed my writing craft I may decide to write a history of Norfolk Island.'

'Oh Meg, I saw men in rags, grey and grim, shivering with cold, chained together on work gangs and poorly fed. All the light had been drained from their eyes. Rupert showed me metal rings attached to the prison walls, where men were tortured by being cuffed, arms and legs spread apart, to a cold wall for hours. A tube gag made from a piece of ironwood was often inserted into their mouths, to stifle their cries of pain. Only a small hole was allowed for breathing. Prisoners slept in rows of hammocks with 20 to 120 packed into each ward. I witnessed one man being flogged until his back was torn and his blood soaked the ground under his feet. Thank God, the worst of these practices has been stopped. When my work here is complete we will depart from this terrible place. I will take you home with me, back to my beloved Edith and my other daughters as quickly as I can.'

Meg and Father fell silent until they reached their destination just as twilight was beginning to fall. Rupert joined them at the dinner table, a hewn log placed on wooden blocks, where they sat on rustic wooden benches. A simple hot meal was served while the escort marines ate in the kitchen. Meg was led to a tiny room with a single bed, a chair and a small table. Slipping out of her riding habit she splashed some water on her face from a jug and basin and fell into bed, heavy with fatigue. The bedding was clean and comfortable and she quickly drifted into sleep.

A gentle knock on her door awoke Meg as she heard, 'Breakfast will be on the table shortly, Miss.' She joined Father and Rupert for eggs, fried bread, jam and tea.

'This morning we will all ride to Cascade Farm where our work will begin. One of the marines, John Watts, will take you to the place where the waterfall begins, Meg. You can easily walk from there to the beach and jetty. After a picnic lunch you will be driven back here to spend the rest of your day as you wish: resting, reading or writing.'

The cart ride to the farm led them past stands of magnificent pine trees. Slowly the landscape changed to reveal areas of former cropping, the soil untilled and left fallow. Rupert explained, 'Only a few fields were under cultivation here and now that the harvest is over, these will not be replanted. By next year nature will have reclaimed nearly all of the farmland.'

Meg and John began their walk through stretches of overgrown greenery. A small trail led them to the beginnings of Cascade Creek, then onward where its waters joined with those of Broken Bridge Creek. Following the bank, they reached an open space at the edge of a cliff where the cascade plunged directly into the sea below. Meg was overcome as she had never experienced a waterfall of this magnitude before. Making their way toward the beach and jetty, they explored the foreshore before returning for lunch. Meg spent the remainder of her day back at old Government Garden, writing until dinner was served. Father, Rupert and the two marines played cribbage afterward as Meg worked at her knitting near the fireside.

Father's work at Cascade was finished by the following noon, so the cart was packed, a lunch stowed away for a rest stop and the party began its return journey. 'I enjoyed this visit so much,' Meg remarked, 'and I was able to add another of Toby's adventures to my book.'

'And I missed my comfortable bed and home study,' Father replied with a laugh. 'It won't be much longer, Meg, until we can return to Mother and the girls. My work here may even be finished by the end of October instead of late November. We will take everything day-by-day and see how it all works out.'

9

In late May, bitter winds announced the arrival of winter. A fire was burning in the library as Meg and Beth pulled their chairs closer to the hearth.

'Can you stay for lunch, Beth? Afterward we could take a short walk if this wind dies down.'

'I would like that, Meg. And look at this fine piece of knitting you have finished. Annie will be so pleased to receive these two wash cloths. Now that you have learned how to cast on and bind off, knit and purl, make increases and decreases we will start the scarf for your father tomorrow. I'll show you how to knit stripes of different colours. With this cold weather coming on, he will appreciate a warm scarf.'

'When will you be leaving Norfolk Island with your family?'

'We should be sailing to Port Arthur in early July so I only have a few more weeks more in which to see you.'

'Beth, I'll miss you so much when you leave. You've been a wonderful friend.'

'I'll miss you too, Meg, as I don't know anyone at Port Arthur. I just hope someone of my age will be living there. My father is very eager to move back to Van Diemen's Land as he will become the chief commissariat officer for the penal colony there. It's a fine promotion for him.' The girls talked on then enjoyed a brisk walk after lunch.

When Beth left, Meg withdrew into her bedroom. She sat at her desk, re-reading the latest letter from home. It was brimming with happy news about Fanny's wedding. 'I'm so pleased the weather was perfect and how I would have loved to see Fanny. She must have been a beautiful bride. I wish I could have been home for this wonderful family day,' she thought. Her eyes began to fill with tears.

Annie passed her door so Meg decided that the time was right to offer her two wash cloths. 'Annie, can you come into my room for a minute?'

'Here I am, Mistress Meg. What can I do for you?'

'Beth is teaching me how to knit and I've made you two wash cloths. The first one isn't perfect, as you can see a stitch I dropped here, but the second one looks better. Please accept them as a token. You do so much for Father and me.'

'Mistress Meg, I don't know what to say. Nobody has ever given me a gift before. Thank you for your kindness.'

Meg noticed the tears well up in Annie's eyes. For months now, this quiet woman had worked hard to prepare their meals and keep their home clean. She gave unstintingly of her time and always maintained her cheerful disposition.

'Sit down for a moment, Annie. As you know, Kings Town is closing down at the end of this year. Father and I will be leaving in early November. Do you have a place where you can go?'

'I was apprenticed to the wife of Commandant Price when I first came to the settlement with her. After the Commandant and his wife left, I decided to stay on. I knew that you and your father would need a housekeeper to help you.'

'Will you move on to Port Arthur with the others, and work there?' Meg enquired.

'I have a sister who runs an inn with her husband near Port Arthur. They asked me to help out so I'll be joining them before Christmas. I will have my own room and will earn a small wage. It's the best thing for me, to be with my own family again. I'm looking forward so much to working with them.'

'Annie, I'm pleased to learn of your good news. Yes, it is important to be with family and I'm looking forward to seeing my own mother and sisters soon. I miss them very much.' Meg returned to her letter feeling much happier and soon she was hard at work on her manuscript for *Toby's Travels*.

When Father came home for dinner he seemed unusually cheerful.

'Meg, I have two pieces of news to share with you. Do you recall the incident when several convicts and two soldiers stole a whaling boat and rowed out to sea. I have received news that their boat reached the colony of New South Wales. The police have captured all but two of them. Although I don't admire their act of theft, this group did make an incredible voyage. It's a pity the incident ended in this way, particularly since one of the convicts was eligible to receive a pardon. '

'It all came to a sad ending, although I hear that Port Arthur is not as brutal as this place was.' Meg replied. 'And what about your second piece of good news?'

'I've kept the best for last. I have finally found a good chess player who has challenged me to a match set of three games. His name is Lieutenant Nathan Edwards.'

'I've not heard this name before. Has he recently arrived?'

'He came on the last ship. Lieutenant Edwards is a draftsman and a construction materials technician with the Royal Corps of Engineers, the Sappers. His mission is to gather all the working drawings for the homes on Quality Row and the major buildings designed by the Royal Engineers and Architects. These will be returned to the military base in Victoria. It seems there are drawings for two earlier houses that have gone missing, so he will measure these dwellings and recreate their working drawings.'

'It sounds as though he will have a good deal of work to complete before Christmas,' Meg replied.

'I have invited him to have dinner with us on Saturday evening so we can play chess together afterward. I can hardly wait to win a good chess match again!'

'Father, what if he surprises you by being the better player?'

'All the more reason then to carry on the game! You will also enjoy his company, Meg. I liked him very much from the first moment I met him. He is a true officer and a gentleman.'

'I'll tell Annie to prepare dinner for three of us and I will set an elegant table. I'm so happy you found someone to share your love of chess. And why not play afterward at the table in the library, Father? Annie will lay the fire there and I can read as you battle with him for supremacy. May the best man win!'

'What a wonderful idea, Meg. Tomorrow it will be. Yes, I have waited a long time for this moment.'

* * *

'Good evening, Sir. What a pleasure to meet with you both over dinner.' Lieutenant Nathan Edwards, tall and handsome in his dress uniform, casually entered their drawing room.

'I'm delighted you could join us this evening, Lieutenant Edwards. And may I introduce my daughter, Margaret, who has accompanied me to Kings Town.'

'Mistress Margaret, I'm happy to meet you,' he replied with a slight bow.

'Do call me Meg, Lieutenant Edwards, as everyone here does.'

'And we should call you, Nathan, as I suspect we will be seeing more of you over time,' Father suggested.

Over dinner Nathan shared information about his family and interests. 'Unfortunately my father died soon after I began my military career with the Royal Corps of Engineers. I have always been close to my mother, who is not well. I also have an older sister, Bethany. She is a fine pianist and is married with two small children. Although I have qualified myself as a draftsman and construction materials assistant, my dream has always been to study architecture. And in my free time, which isn't often now, I do enjoy painting.'

'Tell us more about your art work, Nathan. What subjects do you draw and paint?' Meg asked.

'I work with water colours and occasionally finish a pencil drawing with ink and a water wash. Landscapes and buildings interest me most, but here on Norfolk Island, painting seascapes is also presenting a possibility. And where do your interests lie, Meg?'

'I enjoy keeping house for Father and acting as his social secretary and companion,' Meg replied.

'Come now, Meg, you have other talents too. Tell Nathan about your writing,' Father interjected.

'I know a publisher in Hobart Town who is interested in my collection of short stories for children. I'm currently working on a manuscript featuring my Toby jug. In *Toby's Travels*, my little jug is a run-about who enjoys many adventures, although he always returns home at the end of each tale.'

'Children would love these stories, Meg. I'm sure they will be published.' Nathan responded with a smile.

'One day, if I feel that I have a talent for writing, I will study formally by correspondence. There is a fine school in London that offers writing tuition in this way. When I return to Hobart Town in a few months time, my Toby stories should be completed,' Meg replied.

After dinner the three moved to the library where the chess board and pieces had been placed on the table. The men began their game as Meg drew close to the fire with her book. A deep silence settled over the room until Father called out, 'Checkmate!' He had easily won the first game. The second game began and took far longer to complete. Finally Nathan announced his win when Father was forced to lay down his king across the board. 'You played a skillful game, Nathan. I see that you will be a difficult opponent to defeat. Shall we play one final game, to declare tonight's winner?'

'Yes, let us begin,' Nathan responded.

On they played and the hour grew late. Meg excused herself then left them to prepare for bed. 'I wonder who will triumph tonight?' she thought. 'No matter what happens, I'm so happy that Father has finally found a worthy opponent.'

The next morning at breakfast Father discussed the evening. 'Meg, he defeated me fair and square. This young man is a keen player but I will meet him again to secure a win for myself. I can't tell you how wonderful it has been to enjoy some challenging playing for a change.'

'I'm pleased for you, Father, and I too would like to see him again. He is interesting, yet sensitive and kind. Perhaps he would show us one of his pictures and he might even listen to a Toby adventure.'

During the morning Meg set off to collect Beth, and they moved on to Rose's sewing circle. The arrival of winter had sent everyone away from the veranda into the drawing room and its cozy fireplace. By now only Rose, Meg, Beth and a new member, an officer's wife named Florence, attended the circle. During their morning tea Beth was asked about her departure.

'We will be leaving in five weeks and already my mother and I are beginning to pack a few items. While I am looking forward to our new location at Port Arthur, I will miss all of you when we say our final good-byes.'

Meg spoke next. 'You will be especially missed by me as I have been fortunate to find a good friend in you, Beth.' Meg took out the scarf that she had just finished. 'I wanted to show this to you all before I present it to my Father.' She held up a long tan scarf with a coloured tweed fleck. The two ends were decorated with several stripes, moving from thick to thin in a royal blue and dark brown. A fringe of three colours completed the edges of the scarf.

'Meg, this is a fine piece of work,' said Rose.

'Your father will enjoy wearing this as it has such a masculine look about it,' Florence replied.

'Beth taught me how to knit and I'll enjoy knitting for many years to come.'

'And I'll keep this circle going for a few more months,' Rose told the group, 'until my husband and I leave the settlement in November. I hope to revive the sewing group again when we reach Port Arthur.'

'May I make a suggestion, Rose? Beth has a birthday coming soon and I'd like to offer our home to celebrate the occasion. We could bring our needlework and afterward enjoy a special morning tea. Beth, your mother should also join us, and I'll send her an invitation.'

Rose was delighted, everyone concurred and the birthday party plans moved ahead. When the day arrived Annie baked her famous scones which she served with jam and cream. Florence brought a fruit cake with thick white icing and Rose provided a platter of dainty sandwiches. All the ladies took their places at the dining table where Meg presided. Birthday presents were not forgotten either as Beth opened gift after gift. Meg had wrapped a new book, "*Mansfield Park*," by Jane Austen. It was one she brought with her to Kings Town and which she signed now to Beth. An enclosed card gave Meg's home address in Hobart Town.

Their last few days together passed too quickly and the time came for the friends to separate. As her ship moved away from Sydney Bay under full sail, Meg remained watching and waving on the quay. Walking back to her home alone, she entered her bedroom to shed a few tears. Yes, she would miss her dear Beth so very much.

10

Nathan arrived on the following Saturday for dinner and an evening of chess. He presented Meg and Father with a framed picture he had drawn in pencil, highlighted in ink, then coloured in by hand. His beautifully rendered drawing represented their house, sketched from outside the front gate. Nathan's addition of colourful flower beds and several tall spruce pines completed its setting. 'This is a memento for you to take back to Hobart Town. I hope it will always serve as a reminder of many happy days spent here on Quality Row.'

'Oh Nathan, this is just superb!' Father declared.

'Thank you for this thoughtful gift. We will always treasure it,' Meg replied.

After dinner, the chess playing began in earnest. Suppressing a smile at the intensity of play, Meg worked on a new piece of knitting. The three games were completed earlier than usual when father announced himself to be the winner. 'I was in good form tonight and now we are even, Nathan. We'll play again in another week.' It made Meg happy to see Father gain such enjoyment from this diversion, particularly when his work was often unrewarding.

On the following day Rupert joined them for their Sunday lunch. As the two men had planned a lengthy afternoon meeting, Meg decided to take a walk. Father cautioned her. 'Meg, don't walk beyond the old cemetery today, as you will be alone and I'd like you to stay near Quality Row.'

'I need some fresh air but I won't be away for long. I will be safe if I stay near our home,' she replied.

As Meg strolled through the old cemetery, she found Nathan looking carefully at the headstones. He spotted her and came over.

'Meg, there are so many stories displayed on these headstones. Some are interesting and others are tragic. What tales all these stones can tell.'

'Nathan, I also enjoy walking here and reading the epitaphs. Let me show you Elizabeth Robertson's grave. She was only twenty-four when she died at Longridge Station and she is the sole member of her family buried here. Her father, Gilbert Robertson, worked as the agricultural superintendant of Longridge Station. The farm is a lovely place to visit.'

After an hour spent in exploring the cemetery and Emily Bay, Nathan offered to escort Meg home. 'Would you mind if I occasionally walked with you on Sunday afternoons, Meg? There are a number of interesting places we could visit that are close by. Your father would also be pleased if you didn't walk alone. Besides, I enjoy talking with you.'

'Yes, Nathan, I'd like this very much. We seem so comfortable in each other's company. Just drop by the front gate and I'll be ready to leave with you.' And so Meg found another walking companion and Father was happy with this arrangement as Nathan would ensure her safety.

Several weeks later, Father asked Meg to join him in the library. 'I have some wonderful news for us, Meg. Sit with me by the fire.'

'Whatever is making you so excited?' she asked. Something was definitely in the air.

'As September approaches, there are only a few prisoners left for me to review, and my paper work is nearly complete. It looks as though we may be able to leave the island by the same ship on which we arrived, the *Fortitude*. It sets sail for Hobart Town in mid-October. Would you be able to see to our packing and be prepared to leave at that time?

'Father, this is wonderful! Yes, I will begin right now to put things in order. I'll write to Mother, Fanny and Emily with this good news, as a ship leaves here in two more days.'

'Before the week is over, Meg, I will have to make a final visit to Longridge Station. There are only a few matters to settle there but they are important. Will you come along with me again, as I feel that you may benefit from a change of scenery?'

'Oh yes! Do count on me for this short trip. I'd love to see the house and gardens one last time.'

'Rupert will travel with us and so will Nathan. He needs to check several dimensions from the main house to amend a drawing. His work here is also nearing completion. When we leave in October, I will take all Nathan's documents and drawings back with us. The Military in Hobart Town requires these materials now. Nathan has also been given clearance to leave the settlement in early November, when he will travel with Mr Withers, the Foreman of Works and his wife, Rose. And so, dear Meg, our time spent here is finally coming to an end.'

Preparations began for the Longridge Station visit when Annie was informed that an overnight stay away from home was forthcoming. Once again she packed a lunch for four people to include: Meg, Father, Rupert and Nathan. On the morning of their departure, a small horse-drawn wagon arrived at the door with Rupert and Nathan leading on horseback. Father helped the two men load a few small items, he assisted Meg into the wagon then joined her. Rupert rode in front while Nathan took up his position at the rear. Meg noticed that both men wore loaded pistols in their holsters. Though there were few convicts left to cause mischief, the sight of their side arms still reassured her. Off they rode into a morning filled with sunshine. The route along Quality Row looked empty, as many of its occupants had left the settlement now. The Longridge Road branched out from Quality Row and within minutes they entered the cool green of a native forest.

On they travelled for nearly an hour, until the familiar large table and benches were sighted under a tall tree. Father called out, 'Let's stop here for a short break and some lunch.' Meg stepped down from the wagon seat to stretch. Nathan carried their food basket to the table. Covering its surface with a cloth, Meg laid out several pieces of fruit and a jug of cool water. Early that morning Annie had baked her delicious soda bread, sliced it and made sandwiches filled with chunks of roast beef or chicken. These were eagerly eaten. After a short rest and a walk to admire the native flora, the party was on its way again.

Finally the fallow fields of Longridge came into view as they made their way up the long drive toward the large elegant homestead. The place was still beautiful but had an empty, desolate air about it. As they reached the entrance, James, the old marine and his wife, Flo came out once again to greet them. 'Welcome to the station again. We heard that this will be your last visit.'

Father replied, 'I'm afraid this is so. We have only some loose ends to tidy up here before the Kings Town settlement will finally close and we will all leave Norfolk Island. Will you both remain here?'

James answered, 'Aye, we will, as a few free settlers and some former convicts, who have completed their sentences, would like to remain. We can grow enough food here to feed ourselves and the small remaining crew left on Quality Row.'

Flo spoke next, 'Come inside now and I'll show you to your rooms. Dinner will be on the table in half an hour as the sun is already setting.' Soon everyone sat around the large dining room table and as always, Flo's cooking didn't disappoint them. After dinner and a quiet walk around the garden, Meg was all too happy to unpack and settle down for the night.

After breakfast the following morning, Meg gathered her writing materials and made her way toward the summer house. Here she would place the finishing touches on the final story of *Toby's Travels*. When she returned to Kings Town she would make a copy of her manuscript, writing carefully with her best penmanship. This would be the copy she would offer to Mr Fossett. Looking outside she noticed Nathan driving pegs into the ground with a wooden hammer, then stretching a measuring tape between the pegs. He would make notes in a small book he carried in his jacket pocket. 'I never thought that I would enjoy the company of a man so much,' she thought. 'Nathan is kind and so comfortable to be with. He is also very handsome, in a strong military way. Am I becoming attracted to him?' Meg mused happily, then returned to her manuscript.

Later that morning Nathan returned and approached the summer house. 'Meg, are you still working here?'

'Yes, I am and it would be good to have some company for a few minutes. '

'May I sit down next to you as I have something I must say, while we have this quiet time alone.'

He took both of her hands in his and looked into her eyes. It felt wonderful being so close to him. 'Meg, I have wanted to ask if you have a special person waiting for you back home in Hobart Town? Is there another in your life - a man that you have promised yourself to?'

'No, there is no other and has never been.'

'Ever since I met you, Meg, I have experienced strong and loving feelings for you. Now I would like to ask if you would allow me to court you, with the possibility that you would consider becoming my wife one day?'

Meg gasped aloud with surprise. 'Nathan, your request has taken my breath away. Because you have asked me openly and honestly, I must answer you in the same way. Ever since we met, you have remained constantly in my thoughts. I appreciate and admire you; your kindness, strength and many talents. Yes, you may court me but I can't imagine how this could happen after we separate. You will be stationed at Botany Bay and I will be living in Hobart Town. '

'Meg, somehow I know I can find a way to be closer to you. But first, let me ask your Father for his permission to court you, before I make any plans. Hearing you agree with me has increased my determination. We will find a way to be together.'

Leaning toward Meg he took her into his arms and held her quietly. Then he kissed her hair, her eyes and finally her lips. 'Never forget, Meg, that I love you.' When she finally opened her eyes he had left but the warmth of his embrace remained with her.

11

Meg's final days were filled with the activity of planning and packing for their departure. 'I can't believe how much I dreaded leaving home and coming to Norfolk Island,' Meg told her Father. 'And now that we are free to return to Mother, Fanny and Emily, I dread leaving Nathan behind. Life is very strange.'

'Meg, I have appreciated the sacrifice you made to help me here and I'm amazed at how much you have matured during these past months. Yet my thoughts are always with Edith, Fanny and Emily. I will be happy to leave Kings Town now and finally go home.'

'Father, when we lived at home you always seemed such a distant figure to me. This was because of your work and the exalted position a father occupies within a family. But since coming here, we have grown closer and I know you so much better now than I did when I was younger.'

'Meg, I have appreciated the opportunity to discover you as a person, with your many fine qualities and talents. All I wish for is that you and Nathan will find happiness together. It is plain to see that you love one another very much.'

All too soon, the *Fortitude* arrived, dropped anchor and was loaded with their belongings. Rose and Florence, Annie, Rupert and Nathan all gathered on the quay to farewell them. As the ship went about and her sails billowed out to capture the wind, Meg blew a final kiss to Nathan before the shore began to recede. The voyage home passed without any major difficulty and soon they were sailing up the Derwent River toward

Constitution Dock in Hobart Town. Edith, Emily, Fanny and William were waiting to greet Meg and Father with cries of joy. 'Welcome home! Thank heaven, you're safely with us at last!'

'Mother, you look beautiful and so much thinner. '

'I must have grown thin with worry about the two of you!'

'Emily, you have matured into a lovely young woman. You must be nearly sixteen now.'

'Oh how I missed you, Meg. And now that I'm older, we can share and do many more things together.'

'Fanny and William, you look so happy. Marriage must agree with you both.'

'We are sharing a lovely secret, Meg. William and I have just learned that I am expecting our first child.'

After the excitement of their homecoming had settled, Meg slipped back into family life once again. All of Nathan's drawings and documentation had been collected by a military courier in Hobart Town, so now Father's duty was completed. Meg began to transcribe the new copy of *Toby's Travels*, and when it was finished she invited Emily to visit the shops with her in Hobart Town. Meg placed her manuscript in Mr Fossett's hands as he eagerly scanned its beautifully written pages. 'Meg, this looks like a fine piece of work. Children will enjoy reading these stories for themselves or having a parent read them aloud. I know an illustrator, a young artist who could create several pictures to print throughout the book. Let me look carefully through everything and I'd like to talk to you again tomorrow afternoon.'

'I'll return tomorrow to discuss any changes you may wish to make.'

'There could be a slight alteration made to the order of these stories and you may also want to include some corrections. I'll see you then, tomorrow.'

Meg returned the following afternoon to hear the good news. 'Meg, I will publish *Toby's Travels*. This is a charming collection and children will enjoy these tales very much. Would you be willing to change the order as I have indicated? Also I've made a few adjustments to several sentences. I think these read much better now. Take a moment to look over my ideas and let me know your thoughts.'

'Mr Fossett, I've looked at everything and I agree with all your suggestions. They do improve the book.'

'Meg, I'll move ahead now with the typesetting and my illustrator is working on four pictures. She has already drawn and coloured a picture of Toby for the front cover. What do you think of it?'

'He looks just like my jug! Yes, this will be perfect.'

'I will sell these stories through my shop here, and at another book store in Botany Bay. You will receive three complimentary copies of your own and a royalty payment of 10% from each sale. I will make this money available to you twice yearly. If you are in agreement, I shall draw up a contract for you and I to sign.'

'Yes, Mr Fossett. This is all so exciting!'

'Congratulations, to you, Meg. You are now a published author!'

Plans for a family Christmas proceeded while Meg met up again with former friends. As her fear of horses had left her, she joined a group for horseback riding through the outskirts of Hobart Town. Meg also contacted the London School of Correspondence to enquire about its literary writing program.

A wonderful family Christmas passed and January arrived but still she had received no news from Nathan. Meg was beginning to worry about him and to wonder if the memories she treasured from their meeting in the Longridge summer house had really happened. 'Perhaps this was all a dream. Could it be possible that Nathan regretted what he had told me and now he doesn't love me or wish to think about me any more? Why doesn't he send a letter? I can't contact him either, as the settlement has now been abandoned and the military have all been located elsewhere?'

In early February Father noticed her distress and spoke quietly to Meg. 'I know you are not happy, Meg, and I'm wondering if Nathan's silence may be the cause of this?'

'Oh Father, I can't understand what happened to change his mind toward me. He told me that he loved me!'

'Meg, I am worried about him too, as it is not in his character to act in this way. I have a well-placed contact within the military. I will suggest to this officer that he enquire about Nathan's whereabouts. Leave this with me, Meg, and I will get back to you with any information I may receive.'

'Thank you, Father. I appreciate this so very much,' Meg replied through her tears.

Two weeks later Father called Meg into the library with the news she had been longing to hear. 'Meg, Nathan is alive, but is not well. He is still recovering in the Botany Bay Military Hospital.'

'He is alive but recovering? Oh, whatever has happened to him?' she cried aloud.

'During the final transportation of prisoners just before Nathan was due to leave, there was an incident that involved him. It seems that a soldier left his pistol unguarded on the table for a brief moment. It was long enough for one of the convicts to snatch the gun and threaten the two soldiers.'

Father told her that the convict shouted, 'Don't try to stop me! I won't go to another penal settlement again. I'll kill both of you first. I'm heading into the wilderness to live as a bushranger. I will only leave here as a free man or a dead prisoner.'

Father continued, 'At that moment one of the soldiers rushed toward the prisoner just as Nathan came through the door. He saw the problem and grasped the prisoner's arm, twisting it as the pistol discharged. The bullet struck Nathan on his right shoulder. It broke his collar bone and came out through his back. Nathan bled profusely but thankfully his shoulder and arm weren't shattered. Meanwhile the two soldiers restrained the prisoner, who was led away in chains. Nathan was brought immediately to the Kings Town Military Hospital where his wound was treated. Unfortunately the wound had become so badly infected that they held the departing ship back for him. The voyage made a first stop at Botany Bay where Nathan was transferred to a larger and better equipped military hospital. He is finally healing well after a long period of painful treatment and recuperation.'

'Oh, what a terrible series of events he has been through! Would I be allowed to write to him?'

'I have secured his address and I know he would want to hear from you as soon as you can write. I will arrange for a military courier to take your letter to Botany Bay, as it will reach him there much sooner.'

'Father, I'll be ever grateful for your help and I'll write immediately. We must send my letter this afternoon.'

'There is another thing I almost forgot to mention. Nathan has been awarded a citation and a medal for bravery. His quick thinking saved the life of a fellow soldier. However he has been officially classified as wounded in action, so he may be required to accept a medical discharge. Although he will be fit for civilian life, he may not be eligible now for a military career.'

Meg's letter was written and dispatched as quickly as she could finish it, and her life moved on as she waited for Nathan's response. Finally Mother knocked on her door calling out, 'Meg, you have just received a letter and small package. It has arrived by military courier.'

'I'm coming, Mother. It must be from Nathan!'

Meg held the package and letter tightly, pressing them to herself. 'It is from Nathan, Mother, although his writing looks so shaky. I wish to read it alone in the library.' Trembling, Meg opened her letter and read its contents.

My beloved Meg,

By now, you and your family will have received the news regarding my accident on Norfolk Island. It has taken a long time for me to recover enough to be able to write to you. I know you will understand and forgive me for not responding. Just as I was beginning to sit up and use my arm, Bethany informed me that our dear Mother had died. You know how much my Mother meant to me. I was heart-broken when I could neither say good bye to her, nor attend her funeral. Mother gave several of her precious items to Bethany, to pass on to me as a personal remembrance. Among them was an antique brooch, belonging to her maternal grandmother. This piece has remained in my family for many years. I have enclosed it in the little box you are probably holding now. It is yours, my precious Meg. Please think of me as you wear it. Let it be a token of my intention to meet you soon and eventually, to make you my wife. I think of you so often and I hope all is well with you and your family.

With all my love,

Nathan

Trembling Meg untied the string around the box. She lifted its cover where a small object lay enfolded in a square of silk. Carefully un-wrapping the piece and holding it her hands, she gazed at an exquisite antique Italian brooch. Against its background of deep blue sapphire, a delicate ivory carving of a woman's profile rested. Around the outside edge, a dozen small diamonds framed a band of ornately wrought silver. The cameo brooch sparkled in the sunlight as Meg pinned it to the centre of her lace collar.

'My dearest Nathan, thank heaven you are alive, you are well, and I will see you sometime soon. Thank you for this beautiful gift, from the bottom of my heart.'

12

At last he came, turning up unannounced at Meg's home. 'I was prepared to camp here as I waited for you on your front doorstep, until you let me come in.' Laughing he took her into his arms, whirled her around and kissed her until Edith appeared and a blushing Meg introduced them.

'You are wearing a business suit instead of your uniform? Have you left the Corps of Royal Engineers?'

'Yes, I was awarded a military discharge so now I am a free man. Remember, Meg, when I told you I would find a way to be near you again? Well here I am, but not quite in the way I had planned. The good news is that I am employed as a draftsman right here in Hobart Town. I am working for a firm of architects and engineers while also beginning my study of architecture. Another of my dreams is being fulfilled.'

Father arrived and the two men joyfully embraced one another. 'So you've come back, Nathan. Now I can defeat you again in a chess match.' Emily appeared and was introduced. In time Nathan also met Fanny and William. Many happy family gatherings were celebrated as Meg and Nathan began their courtship.

A few months later Edith emerged from the sitting room one afternoon, closed the door behind her and leaned back against it with a sigh of relief. Smiling she held her arms out to her daughter calling to her, 'Emily, everything has been settled. Meg is going to be married.'

'The Trousseau'

Paris, Autumn 1864

Excitement filled a beautifully appointed room as morning sunlight slanted through its windows. The Empress Eugenie had gathered five elegantly dressed ladies around a large polished oak table. It was covered with swatches of cotton and printed muslin fabric, scraps of lace, ribbons, writing papers, and toiletries. A sturdy medium-sized sea chest served as the centrepiece.

'I've called you all together to help me solve a problem.' Eugenie addressed those present: the Princess d'Essling, her chief Lady-in-Waiting, her wardrobe mistress and her two dressmakers.

The ladies laughed lightly as they greeted each other, kissed one another's cheeks and took their places. 'I love solving a problem, especially if it has something to do with a woman's wardrobe,' the Princess replied.

After all had been seated Eugenie spoke. 'If you were a young bride leaving France to sail to an island in the far South Pacific Ocean, never to return home again, what would you pack in your trousseau?'

A gasp was heard around the table. 'Now please take a moment to think on this then we'll hear from each of you.' As the surprised group looked silently at the table Eugenie sat back, reflecting on the unusual circumstances that required her to hold this meeting.

During the previous summer, Louis Napoleon Bonaparte, now Emperor Napoleon III, observed two footmen as they carried an ornate silver tray to his mahogany desk. In the centre of the tray rested a large, well scrubbed rock. Louis had carefully selected this space so that full sunlight bathed the rock in a golden glow. On its surface many large veins of iridescent green and deep blue took on a sparkling sheen, so beautiful, that he caught his breath whenever he looked at it.

'You may leave now,' he told the footmen. Louis then smiled at an elegant woman who had just entered the room.

'Join me over here, Eugenie. I have something amazing to show you!' The Empress Eugenie, his beautiful consort, quickly crossed the floor and gazed in wonder at the shimmering rock.

'What is this? Have you found an emerald in the stone?'

'No, this rock contains nickel and has just come from the island of Grande Terre in the South Pacific.'

'Where is this place and what is nickel used for?'

'In 1853 this island became a French possession to serve as a penal colony. But vast amounts of nickel have also been discovered in underground caves and rocks everywhere. When nickel is mined the mineral has many uses. It strengthens coins, it is ideal for plating iron and brass and this beautiful green provides an emerald tint for glass making. In addition cobalt can also be extracted from the rock and used for its rich blue colouring.'

'This could be of benefit to all our painters and glass artisans, particularly those who make our stained glass windows.'

'Now please be seated, Eugenie, as I have a plan to discuss with you. I must turn to you again as you always offer me the best advice.'

Louis then explained that Grande Terre, soon to be called Nouvelle-Caledonie, had to be colonized and the French presence strengthened, so as to thwart attempts by the British to seize or steal away its valuable minerals.

'Last year we transported a ship filled with our first convicts and some political prisoners to the island. A group of free settlers are in residence there as well. Many of the convicts are young men who have been sentenced for very minor offences. After these men serve out their sentences the French Government will offer them a free parcel of land, should they choose to stay. Already there is a small settlement being built on the south west of the island around a chain of beautiful bays. It is known today as Port-de-France. However the most essential part of this colonial program is missing. All these men will need wives – strong young women who will marry them and raise children for France. Please think on this as I know you will find a way to invite young women to our noble calling. Yes, our Grande Terre settlement plan now demands your woman's touch.'

'Louis, I already have the spark of an idea growing in my mind and I will give my full attention to your request. Leave this now with me.'

Eugenie had always found practical solutions for any requests made of her and she enjoyed planning ways to better the lives of French women, particularly those of the poor classes. This new challenge, involving an island paradise in the South Pacific, captured her imagination and would become a special project on which to work.

* * *

In another part of Paris three young girls, Clotilde, Louise and Jeanne, were on their hands and knees singing happily. They had just finished scrubbing a hallway of hewn slate. It was a tedious job, keeping the entrance and main hall of the Mater Dei Orphanage clean and sparkling. Over the years the girls had become close friends and they enjoyed singing as a way to lighten their load.

'Well done, girls,' called Sister Celeste as she inspected their work. 'After you have finished your cleaning, meet me in the large room for reading and numbers.'

All the girls at the Mater Dei home loved Sister Celeste. She was gentle and kind often interceding for them after a sharp scolding from Mother Germain. The home housed many young orphans ranging in age from infants to girls in their late teens. All of them worked in some way toward maintaining the smooth running of the orphanage. The older girls were skilled in cooking, cleaning, washing, sewing and caring for each young child. In exchange for their work they were well fed, taught to pray and to read, to do their numbers and to excel in needlework. As they matured the sisters found placements for their charges in the homes of their wealthy benefactors.

'If you need a perfect housemaid or even a governess, choose one from the Mater Dei,' the women of Paris often said. 'This orphanage turns out only the finest girls.'

Yet Mother Germain and her sisters were concerned as the numbers of older girls kept increasing. It was also becoming more difficult to find placements for them.

'Dear sisters, we have a problem with the numbers of our older girls. Several of them should be moved away now from Mater Dei. You are all aware that we carefully place these girls in homes or institutions that always have their highest good in mind.' Mother Germain spoke to her community during an urgent meeting.

'We must never send them away to find suitable work on their own. Perhaps we could involve the Archbishop in our concerns, as he may provide an answer to our present difficulty,' Sister Celeste suggested.

After several others spoke they prayed together for a solution to the problem, as help was needed during this challenging time.

2

Late in November of 1864 flurries of snow had begun to cover the ground in a blanket of white. Eugenie watched this first sign of approaching winter from her large windows as the footmen heaped more wood on the fire. Moments later another footman appeared carrying a sturdily built sea chest. It was too large for a woman to carry alone but easy for a man to lift.

'Please place it on the mahogany table in the centre of the room,' Eugenie instructed him.

Then excitedly she opened the lid and its contents became visible, just as the Emperor entered the room.

'Louis, I have been busy at work on our Grande Terre project and I've accomplished much to share with you. Over the past month I have visited several orphanages and spoken to the Reverend Mothers and sisters. There are numerous girls who are entering marriageable age and may be interested in volunteering for the voyage to Grande Terre. Together we assembled a list of the following requirements for each of the girls: they must be no younger than sixteen years of age and they must realize that they go to be married and to bear children for France and the Church. They must also promise to remain on Grande Terre. Am I correct to say that their French citizenship will be continued for them, their husbands and children?'

'Of course, they will always remain citizens of France.'

Eugenie continued, 'The young women will sail from France shortly before Easter of next year and each of the girls will be presented with an early wedding gift from me, her own personal trousseau. I have assembled this little gift here on the table and invite you to inspect its contents.'

'Eugenie, I'm amazed. You have achieved so much in such a short time. Now let me see what you have cleverly packed into this charming little chest.'

Eugenie then proceeded to lift out the first layer which contained an opened box. Placed inside were all the essentials to make a young woman feel cherished and beautiful: an ivory hand mirror, a matching hair brush and comb, a bar of perfumed soap tied with satin ribbon, scented face crème and one small bottle of cologne. A hand written card rested on the top bearing the notation: *With best wishes from the Empress Eugenie.*

'Oh, how appropriate for a trousseau!' exclaimed the Emperor. 'This is so feminine and will be certain to attract the attention of any young girl.'

'But wait, Louis, as there is more to come.'

Eugenie then proceeded to lift out a long white cotton dress beautifully embroidered with tiny flowers and trimmed with lace. 'See how cleverly the dress falls from a square yoke and elbow length gathered sleeves. It should fit all sizes of our little French brides – large and small. And to complete the wedding ensemble is a simple shoulder length lace veil attached to a white embroidered head band.'

'Magnificent,' he replied.

At the bottom of the chest rested two towels, a sewing kit and a manicure set. A beautifully bound New Testament and a folder of writing papers with pens, pencils and ink completed the contents.

'You and your committee are to be congratulated, Eugenie. You have all excelled yourselves.'

'If this meets with your approval we should begin to interview the girls before Christmas so that each trousseau can be completed on time. The ships must also be fitted out with extra supplies of bedding, crockery, cutlery and cooking utensils to give them all a good start with their home-making. The girls know how to read, do numbers, cook, sew and take care of children. They are also well taught in matters of the Catholic faith so they should make fine wives and mothers.'

'Eugenie, you have found the perfect solution; and to have packed this complete trousseau into a sea chest – inspirational! Yes, we must proceed immediately by sending a sample of each trousseau to the various orphanages. I'd like to see at least twelve girls ready to sail by the end of March, next year.' And so the plan began to move ahead.

* * *

A buzz of excitement always filled Mater Dei in the weeks before Christmas. Many gifts were wrapped, thoughtfully provided by the benefactors, so every child would find something for themselves under the Christmas tree. Carols and hymns of the season were practiced for the midnight mass and the delicious scent of Christmas cakes and puddings wafted through the hallways. But the main source of excitement was a coming meeting, to be conducted by the Archbishop himself and Mother Germain. All of the girls who were sixteen years of age and over were requested to attend. Whatever could this be about?

Finally the afternoon for the meeting arrived as the girls and Mother Germain, surrounded by many of the sisters, gathered in the large chapter room. Seated in an armchair against the centre of the main wall sat the Archbishop, resplendent in his purple satin robes and skull cap. After Mother Germain greeted him and kissed his ring of office, all of the girls curtseyed in unison. Then the Archbishop rose and spoke to all of those present.

'I have in my hands an invitation from the Emperor Napoleon III and Empress Eugenie. They are inviting all interested young girls to sail from France to the beautiful island of Grande Terre, far away in the Pacific Ocean. It is their wish that you would leave here to become brides, wives and mothers for the Glory of France and the Church.'

The conditions were then read aloud. Each girl was instructed to think and pray very carefully before she made her decision. Mother Germain would present him with a list of the volunteers on the third day after Christmas. The young girls were thunderstruck!

'But before you leave the room we have a surprise for you. The Empress Eugenie has prepared a gift for each one of you who chooses to make the voyage.'

Mother Germain then went over to a sea chest displayed on a table nearby. She faced the girls and told them that each one would receive a trousseau for herself, just like this one. Mother Germain then proceeded to unpack and display the entire contents of the chest, raising each exquisite item aloft for all to see. Gasps of amazement were heard filling the room together with cries of 'Ooh,' and 'Ah,' growing ever more frequent. When she had finished Reverend Mother again told the girls they were to consider this offer very carefully and in the coming three days she would meet with those who wished to volunteer.

'Remember that you will be leaving France for the rest of your lives, sailing on a journey toward marriage and motherhood. It will not be easy. You will all experience happy events and great hardships. Parts of the island may even be dangerous. Feel free to discuss this with one another. Pray to Mother Mary and to your guardian angel. Sister Celeste will also answer all your questions as I know how fond you are of her. Now bow to the Archbishop, and then you may leave.'

A deep silence settled over the Mater Dei dining room during the dinner and continued into the evening. Small groups began to gather and discuss the events of the day with muted questions. Worries were shared. Excitement at the magnitude of this adventure was expressed, together with the future of becoming a wife and mother. After the lights were turned out they tossed and turned in their beds, barely able to sleep during that long night. As bright sunshine welcomed everyone the next morning, each of the girls had arrived at her decision. After breakfast Louise, Jeanne and Clotilde found each other. Hugging they asked the question that could be heard on every pair of lips.

'Will you be leaving?'

'Yes, I am going to Grande Terre. I have no family here and if I leave I will have a chance to make a family of my own,' Clotilde answered.

'I am also leaving France for the Pacific Island,' said Louise. 'My days will be filled with excitement and adventure instead of all this dreary work and study.'

'I will remain right here as I am happy at the orphanage and I hope one day to work in a fine house.

Anyway, I'm afraid of the big open sea,' Jeanne spoke firmly.

One of the girls in a group of onlookers, Satine, overheard the three and joined them.

'I have also decided to make the long journey. Perhaps I will find someone there I could marry – one who would make a home and family with me.'

By the next afternoon three girls: Clotilde, Louise and Satine told Mother Germain that they would be happy and honoured to make the long journey to Grande Terre. There was much work to be finished and items for packing to be considered.

Then finally in late March of 1865, the fateful day arrived for the young brides-to-be to say their tearful farewells and prepare to set sail. In all, nine young women presented themselves at portside, each to collect her personal trousseau and go aboard. The Grande Terre project had achieved a small but successful beginning and over the coming years many more young French women would follow in the footsteps of these first courageous travelers. No one was happier, than Louis Napoleon and Eugenie. After all, it was her thoughtful plan and 'woman's touch' that had saved Grande Terre and its vast nickel deposits for the Glory of France.

3

Time had flown by since the nine young brides-to-be met one another at the port of Brest, to board the barquentine that would sail them halfway around the world. The days were growing warm and sunny and thankfully the sea was calm, allowing each of them a chance to grow accustomed to the endless rise and fall of the ship. The young women were bunked together in a section of the lower deck and a cloth curtain separated them from the other passengers. Two family groups were also aboard - officers of the French Army with their wives and children. Several men engaged in the business of trade; Father Gilbert, a Marist priest; and a small contingent of young soldiers completed the passenger list.

Within three weeks they had sailed past France and Portugal and were approaching the Madeira Islands, off the northwest coast of Africa. Here they would stop to take on fresh supplies. By then all the passengers had met one another and merged into a friendly group of travel companions. Louise, in her outgoing adventurous way, had made the acquaintance of all the passengers. But much to Clotilde's consternation, Louise was now spending nearly all of her time with a handsome young man, a passenger who had also boarded at Brest.

'Clotilde and Satine, I'd like you to meet Raoul Cortega. He lives on Madeira Island where his grandfather owns one of the largest wineries. His family makes the famous Madeira and port wines and Raoul is bringing back new rootstock for his grandfather to plant.'

He greeted the girls pleasantly in perfect French. 'You are surprised that I speak French? My mother is from Nice and my father is Portuguese so both languages are spoken in my home. Come along with me and I'll show you my precious cargo.'

The four went below where Raoul pointed out his ten carefully wrapped, large twisted roots. 'Look at how I've covered them all in wet burlap. Every other day I must turn them, check carefully and occasionally pour water over them. If the rootstock dries out, these Bastardo and Muscat grape roots will not transplant well. We will reach Porto Funchal in a short time and I'll be leaving the ship there with my stock.'

'This is Raoul's third trip away from Madeira to buy these plants,' Louise interjected. 'He is becoming a seasoned traveler.'

'But let me say this is the first time I've made the journey to France for new rootstock. Usually I purchase grape vines from Spain or Portugal. It has been such a pleasure to meet Louise and now, her two travelling companions.' Raoul nodded to them.

'We are on our way to Grande Terre, at the invitation of Emperor Napoleon and Empress Eugenie,' Clotilde spoke. 'Our presence will help to secure this settlement for France.'

Satine added, 'We all chose to make this voyage and I am looking forward to all the places we will visit. I have never seen anything outside of the Mater Dei Orphanage before this day.'

'I wish you both a happy future on your new island home,' answered Raoul. He looked fondly at Louise then bowed to them as he left the group.

After a few more days of sailing, land was sighted and the ship docked at Funchal. What a joy is was, to leave the confines of the ship and move around again on firm land.

'I have to learn how to walk all over again. It feels so strange not to be moving up and down,' Satine remarked.

Clotilde brought over two other young women who had become friendly with them. 'Let's all go out together in this beautiful warm sunshine and explore Funchal,' she suggested. 'Aren't we lucky to have three days of freedom on dry land?'

'Will Louise join us too?' asked Marianne, one of the girls.

'I can't seem to find her,' Clotilde replied, 'but let's be off now. We may even meet her along the way.'

Funchal appeared so exotic and beautiful to the eyes of these young women who had only known Paris from the interior of an orphanage. Their first shock came amidst the vibrant colours and abundant array of spring flowers: lilies, orchids, gazanias and a strange plant with a beak-like structure growing from its flower.

'Someone told me it is called, Bird of Paradise,' Marianne spoke amidst their laughter. The decorative paved streets looked miraculous. The stone shops and buildings had brightly coloured roofs and everything was so clean, fresh and vibrant. The first day passed quickly and soon it was time to go back on board again for the evening meal.

On the second day Raoul offered to take Louise and the group on a tour of Funchal's civic buildings. He told them wonderful stories about the Madeira Islands. They particularly loved the tale about the famous English pirate, William Kidd, whose ship had sunk close to one of the deserted small islands. The wreckage of his ship had never been found although many were still searching for it.

'One day, someone will discover this ship and claim the immense treasure that sank with her,' Raoul told them. 'It won't be me though as I'll be kept busy at the winery. There is always so much work to do there.'

'Look at that unusual building down near our ship. What is it used for?' Satine asked.

'That is St Tiago's Fort. It was built two hundred years ago to protect the city from pirates,' Raul replied. Next to it is the customs house, just over behind me is the cathedral and next to that, the convent of Saint Clare.'

'Let's visit the cathedral before we return to the ship,' Clotilde called out. 'It looks so beautiful and we'll have just enough time.'

The cathedral was cool and quiet as they prayed then moved around its interior, admiring the carved cedar ceiling inlaid with ivory and the magnificent Flemish and Portuguese paintings behind the ornate Baroque altar. A young nun overheard them whispering in French and approached them.

'Greetings. I am Sister Veronica and I welcome you to Funchal.'

'Oh, what a pleasant surprise! You speak French,' the girls replied.

'Yes, my family came here from France years ago, but most of the sisters here speak only Portuguese. When do you sail and where are you going?'

'Tomorrow is our last day here in port and we must return to the ship by late afternoon so that we can sail out before sunset. We are bound for the island of Grande Terre,' Clotilde replied.

Sister Veronica interjected, 'Oh do come to the convent tomorrow for lunch and visit us before you leave. We can all meet you and learn about your long voyage to Grande Terre and why you are making this journey.'

Raoul then added, 'I'm sure all these young women would enjoy a visit with you and the sisters. I must stay on the ship, to make sure my cargo is unloaded safely so that I can leave during the afternoon when my coach arrives.'

And so it was decided. On the final day in port Clotilde, Louise and Satine slipped into their Sunday dresses and enjoyed a light lunch at the convent. Sister Veronica acted as their interpreter. There was much news to share and stories about Mater Dei to be told as the time passed quickly. The girls completed their visit with a tour of the convent's beautiful Baroque chapel and finally the cloister gardens, to admire the herbs and flowers that grew in abundance.

'Thank you, for your hospitality and this lovely day,' all replied as they embraced the sisters and made their way back to the ship. It had been a perfect finish to their first port of call.

Late in the afternoon as everyone gathered in the wardroom before their evening meal, the ship prepared to set sail for the second leg of their journey. Louise appeared briefly and then excused herself.

'I'd like to rest for a while and then go out on deck for some fresh air. I don't feel well,' said Louise.

'We'll see you later,' Clotilde called out to her.

When they finished their dinner they felt a slow lurching movement of the ship as it began to leave. All moved out on deck to admire the rising moon and watch the port slowly fade behind them into the distance. They laughed and talked quietly among themselves until Clotilde suddenly felt very tired. All the others, too, began to leave for bed.

'I'll see Louise in the morning,' thought Clotilde. 'I am sure she is feeling well by now and is probably sound asleep.' Clotilde climbed into her bunk, dozed lightly then sank into a deep slumber.

Only the following morning after they were well on their way, did Clotilde first notice Louise's empty bed. Only then did she see that her trousseau was missing from its place on the floor. It was at that same moment that she found a note and read its contents. The tears began to stream down her cheeks.

Satine suddenly joined her, crying aloud in consternation, 'Clotilde, I'm very worried. Where is Louise? I've looked everywhere for her!'

'Sit next to me, Satine. I have something I must share with you.'

'You've been crying, Clotilde. Something dreadful must have happened?'

'I have some very distressing news from Louise. She has left a letter for the two of us.'

Clotilde showed Satine a note written in Louise's handwriting. Both of them took a deep breath as Satine drew close to Clotilde, their arms around each other. Clotilde read its message aloud through her tears.

Dear Clotilde and Satine,

By the time you read this note you will be sailing toward Cape Town. I decided to leave the ship in Madeira to stay with Raoul. He has asked me to marry him and we plan to live outside Funchal on his grandfather's winery. I will miss you both and I know that you will find happiness in Grande Terre. Don't be angry with me. I love Raoul and have decided to follow my heart. I pray that you, Mother Germain and the Archbishop will forgive me. I will write to the sisters at Mater Dei and I will never forget you.

Your loving friend,

Louise

The two girls were speechless with shock and surprise. Satine spoke first.

'Clotilde, she promised Mother Germain and the Archbishop she would sail to Grande Terre. She accepted the gift from the Empress, but she deceived us all.'

'Satine, I too am very saddened but we must not stand in judgement on Louise. We will tell the ship's captain what has happened, show him the note and then pray for her. I want Louise to have a happy life with Raoul.'

'We will never see Louise again.' Satine began to cry as the two sat quietly, holding hands and speaking in whispers, about the past events of their voyage. At least they were still together, able to offer comfort and friendship to each other through the time of their first loss.

4

On a late October morning a cry rang out over the barquentine.

'Land Ho!' Clotilde awoke with a start to hear the call again.

By now many were dressing quickly and hurrying to the port side, to gaze at a thin sliver of green that was barely seen against the horizon. The sun was rising in the east, its brilliance creating a pathway of molten gold. The sea was calm and the possibility of an end to their journey filled everyone's hearts with exultation.

'Ladies and gentlemen, Grande Terre lies ahead, two days sailing on our present course.' Captain LaValle's voice rang out loudly over the ship and the passengers broke into shouts of joy and loud clapping. At last, after seven long months as sea, the voyage would finally be over. Clotilde and Satine hugged each other as they shared their excitement.

'Finally we can leave the confines of this cramped, dark ship and get away from the constant rolling of the sea. I can hardly wait to take a bath again and wear some clean clothing.'

'I'm longing to have some space for a good walk on land again as well as fresh food and water. Everything tastes so stale now and this morning the bread at breakfast was filled with weevils.'

Their previous two stopovers at Cape Town in South Africa and Batavia in Java had offered a welcome relief from sailing. The first view of the port at Table Bay included the wrecks of several ships. Only four jetties were operational here and the waterfront had become cluttered with skin-drying, wool-processing, fish-smoking and boat-building establishments. There was little to see in Cape Town other than the Castle of Good Hope and several buildings of architectural beauty. Yet a major stopover here of several days allowed everyone to go ashore again, to break the monotony of sailing and to replenish supplies. The voyage resumed, the Cape of Good Hope was passed and only the last leg of the journey remained.

Their final stop in Batavia was the most welcome one of all. This small but very prosperous settlement functioned as the headquarters for the Dutch East India Company. The settlement was administered within the walls of Batavia Castle, where a thriving trade in silk, tea and spices continued to flourish. Outside the castle, on spacious avenues lined with tall shade trees, lived the wealthy Dutch merchants and their families. Their elegant two-storey homes, built of white timber and stone, lined these roadways. There was much to enjoy here as the passengers walked through the castle, the harbour fortifications and splendid avenues. It was good to do some shopping and stretch their land legs again.

'I'm happy to spend a few days here although the weather is very hot and humid,' Satine mentioned.

'I hope Grande Terre will be settled as well as Batavia is,' replied Clotilde.

The ship's stores were replenished with fresh water and more supplies. Then the last stage of the journey began, down the north-eastern coast of the Great South Land to Grande Terre.

By now Clotilde felt a deep sense of joy because she had received a special acknowledgement. It was earned on board the ship, through her own hard work. She had unknowingly put an event into motion that had secured a fine position for herself on Grande Terre and it made her heart sing. This event began after the shock of Louise's departure had worn away and the voyage resumed, sailing along the coast of Africa toward Cape Town.

By now Clotilde and Satine had met the two families that accompanied the officers. One young wife named Blandine had three children – eight and six year old boys and a beautiful baby girl. The other family, Lucie's children, included a seven year old girl and a five year old boy. As their journey ground motonously on the children had grown restless. Of late the boys had become a nuisance on the ship, running up and down the deck, laughing loudly and climbing over ropes and boxes. Finally Captain LaValle complained to their fathers.

'I don't know what to do with them any more either,' their tired mothers chorused. 'They need something to occupy their time and settle them down.' Clotilde noticed this too and an idea entered her mind. She approached both mothers the next day.

'I see that you have several story books on the shelf above your stored trunks. Let me take them and I'll gather the children for story-reading time in the mornings.'

'What a wonderful idea, Clotilde.'

Much to everyone's relief the children loved their story time with Clotilde, who read to them in a warm and lilting voice, frequently asking questions about each story and the interesting animals and people found in it. The story sessions then expanded as wooden pencils and paper, reading books, slates and chalks were offered. Blandine, Lucie and Clotilde approached Captain LaValle, to request some table space in the ship's wardroom during the late mornings and early afternoons. He was delighted to oblige them and soon regular schooling had begun.

To her surprise, Clotilde discovered that she had a talent for teaching. On many occasions she recalled the classes Sister Celeste had taught them at Mater Dei. Sister would explain a new lesson to the group, then as the girls worked at their desks, she would move around, checking carefully to make sure they understood what they were doing. Those who were slow to master the lesson were called up to her desk for extra practice. Older girls always helped the younger ones, and only when all were ready, did Sister Celeste move ahead to something new. Clotilde had a kind and compassionate mentor – the perfect model for her own style of teaching. It proved very successful as the children loved her. Clotilde was firm, but always patient. Little by little, working away in the semi-darkness of the wardroom, on the table that rose and fell with the rhythm of the waves, the children began to improve their skills in reading, writing and arithmetic.

Then Satine stepped forward with a welcome suggestion. 'When I was at Mater Dei, Sister Aimee taught me how to play the piano. Let me take the children for a short singing lesson. I can teach them some of our French hymns and folk songs.' In no time the children and their mothers had formed a choir. Satine had a beautiful soprano voice and when Captain

LaValle heard them singing, he offered her an old pump-organ which she accepted with delight.

'We have a small harmonium in the officer's wardroom that has been covered with a cloth for ages. No one could ever play it, but perhaps it may be useful to you, Satine, and to my floating classroom.'

She found three notes that wouldn't sound and the organ wheezed badly when she pumped the two pedals. After the ship's carpenter made repairs and reattached the bellows, it was brought back into working order once again. Satine was thrilled and produced her only book – a French hymn book - bound in leather and presented to her by Sister Aimee when she left for Grande Terre. She played accompaniments for the choir and provided music for Father Gilbert's Sunday morning mass, celebrated for all on the foredeck. On one special Sunday feast day as the choir sang, Satine's angelic soprano floated above on a second line of melody. The entire ship's company clapped and cheered her when she had finished. Satine was so overwhelmed she burst into tears on the spot.

And now, at last, after the welcome cry of, 'Land Ho!' their long voyage was finally coming to its end. Clotilde, Satine, the mothers and pupils rehearsed for the concert they would present on their last evening at sea. Everyone gathered on the deck as twilight slowly descended. It was a balmy, magical night as a new moon began to rise slowly beneath a canopy of shining stars. Captain LaValle addressed all present.

'We have endured a long voyage together and I wish to express my thanks to one and all, for making this journey a safe and happy one.'

The captain was given three resounding cheers. Father Gilbert then gave everyone a final blessing after which all sang a hymn. The choir presented two French folk songs. Satine was invited to stand as she was presented with a lovely silk shawl by Lucie. There was much applause. For their final offering the children recited a poem from memory and acted in a little play they had written, based upon one of their stories. Each child had a part and not one forgot their lines. They were thrilled to have done so well.

At the conclusion of the farewell concert the two officers and their wives requested that Clotilde now step forward. As she faced the entire ship's company - captain, crew and passengers, they thanked her for her many hours spent in teaching their children. Blandine presented her with a gift of their appreciation – a beautiful black onyx inkstand and holder, together with a wooden pen. Its writing end was bound with leather and decorated with a small gold band. In a second box were four steel nibs and a bottle of ink. An officer spoke.

'Our dear Clotilde, may this gift grace your desk, as we extend our invitation to you, to teach the children of our Government and Military at Grande Terre. We have learned that a teacher is badly needed there. One was to sail with us, but at the last moment she decided not to join us on this voyage. We were all distressed until you stepped forward to teach our children. You will have thirteen pupils in all, ranging in age from six to eleven years, including our children. Your skills are greatly in demand and we eagerly await your reply.'

Clotilde was overcome. 'I can be a teacher in my new home,' she thought to herself. 'I will make a place for myself where I will be useful to the colony. Her mind was made up and her reply came then and there.'

'Yes. I thank you for this beautiful gift and I will be honoured to accept your offer.'

A chorus of clapping and cheering followed as Clotilde fought to hold back her tears. They only came later that night when she sat alone on her bunk. They were not tears of sorrow, but of great happiness. The long voyage was safely over. At last she had safely reached her new home.

5

Clotilde was seated at her desk in the school room on a warm Sunday morning in December. Sunlight streamed through the windows reflecting off a small glass vase filled with bright flowers. Spreading out the note paper from her trousseau, beneath her onyx inkstand in its pride of place on the desk, she began writing her first letter from Grande Terre. A supply ship would be leaving for France at the end of the week and it would carry this letter back to Mater Dei. She had so much news to share with Mother Germain and Sister Celeste. Time seemed to fly by as she filled several pages. Then a voice interrupted her.

'Clotilde, here I am at last.' Satine appeared in the doorway and the two young women embraced as they kissed one another on both cheeks.

'I'm so happy you have your Sundays free so we can spend them together,' replied Clotilde. 'Let's go back into my little garden where I've set the table for our lunch.'

'Something smells delicious! You've made us onion soup, with bread and cheese.' Laughing and chatting they said grace then began to eat.

'Satine, you must tell me about how you are enjoying your days as a governess? When I attended my first Sunday mass I was amazed to see you take your place at the pipe organ and lead us in the hymns. Your playing sounded so beautiful.'

'When my turn came to meet with the committee, imagine my surprise when Father Gilbert was there to introduce me to Madame Fleurier, the commandant's wife.'

'And what did she say to you?' Clotilde queried.

Madame said, 'News of your musical ability has already reached me, Satine, and I have the only piano here at Port-de-France in our home. Our two daughters are still too young to attend the school but both are eager to learn about music. They will also need the care and supervision of a governess for several more years. And our Church of Saint Joan has no organist. Would you be willing to live in our home and undertake these duties: caring for our two young girls, offering occasional piano lessons and playing for our Sunday masses? You will have a large bedroom of your own, a small sitting room and the use of our library and garden. Sunday and Wednesday afternoons will be yours to spend as you wish. Does this interest you?'

'I was so pleased with her offer that I said then and there, Madame Fleurier, I will be very happy to accept this and I will do my best to please you and your family. And Father Gilbert, it will be my pleasure to assist you by providing music for the church.'

'I am so delighted you are settled,' Clotilde replied.

'Yes, I am happily employed in a very grand home by a wonderful family. Father Gilbert has also made the organ available to me on Saturday afternoons if I want to practice.'

Both began to reminisce as Satine asked, 'Remember our first days on the island?' They talked about those wonderful days again when they finally left the ship. Waiting for them on the pier were three women and two soldiers, who embraced the eight young travellers as each collected her luggage and trousseau.

'Welcome to Port-de-France. It is our pleasure to greet you today. We are all so happy to see that you have arrived safely.' Soon all were ushered into a large cottage set back off the roadway near the pier. Here the men left them in the care of the reception committee.

'Welcome to all you dear young women. I am Madame LeBec. You have endured a very long and uncomfortable voyage and we have several surprises for you. Come along first to your bedrooms. You will be sharing them, with three of you in each room. Leave your belongings, refresh yourselves and then meet us back in the dining room.'

As they all enjoyed platters of cold meat, fresh fruit, cheese and bread, Fontine, their housemother addressed them.

'You will all want to rest, wash your hair again and have a long hot bath. We have been asked to provide you with soap, hair wash, a nightgown and fresh towels. You will also need some new clothing too, so after lunch our finest dressmakers will measure you for two new white blouses, a day skirt and a muslin Sunday dress. You may each choose the colour and pattern for your new dress from the samples the LeBlanc sisters have brought. We have two sewing machines in the back room so in a day or two you will all look very stylish again. This last thoughtful touch to your homecoming has been provided by the Empress Eugenie herself. She is so grateful to each of you for your decision to settle here on Grande Terre. '

What excitement those first days held as each young woman chose her new dress, trimmed with ribbons and lace. Attired in a fresh blouse and skirt, they set out in small groups to explore the settlement. At this time there were about four hundred people living in Port-de-

France. Along the paved main street were shops selling a variety of goods: clothing, groceries, books, and household items. The back street held a blacksmith shop, a butcher, a shoe maker, harness makers, hardware goods, seeds and weapons. Behind these two business streets were timber cottages built into the hillsides. Each displayed a flower garden near the front door and a well-tended vegetable garden at the back. Often a covered porch enclosed two sides of each cottage. The newly arrived visitors marveled at these open verandas, as they were called. All homes faced the sea that always looked so beautiful when the turquoise hue near the shore turned to cobalt blue in the deeper waters. The entire settlement was planned to cluster around two bays, and an abundance of trees, shrubs and flowers grew everywhere.

'It's not as old or grand as Funchal, but is very lovely in its own way,' Clotilde remarked.

'Port-de-France has a charm and relaxed air about it I find very attractive,' Satine replied. 'Thank goodness it's not as hot as Batavia either and I'm happy now that we've chosen to come here to live.'

The LeBlanc Sisters' dress shop, however, was the magnet that drew them back again and again. On display were samples of finished dresses, hanging on padded hangers or draped across elegant chairs. Shelves were stacked with bolts of lovely soft cottons and muslins, shawls, lace collars and cuffs, ribbons, sewing notions and pieces of jewelry. Madame LeBlanc smilingly enticed them with her irresistible samples.

'Just look at this lace trim with its scalloped edging. Such fine, delicate workmanship! Wouldn't it suit the new muslin print that just arrived?' The girls gathered around her to gaze in wonder.

'Now don't forget that each of you young ladies will receive a wage when you begin your work. Save your money, then come to me. I will dress you in beautiful clothing. All our women must look their best, for is this not the French way?'

As the weather was warm for most of the year dresses had elbow length sleeves, loose at the bottom or gathered above the elbow. Necklines were open just below the throat, and skirts flared from a high fitted bodice or a belted waist. Shawls were very popular and provided a protective mantle for cooler days or evenings. Skirts ended just above the ankle to make gardening and walking through the unpaved back streets easier. Formal wear, also on display was made from satins, brocades and silks, beautifully trimmed with ruffles, tucks and covered buttons. Yet the practical white or coloured blouses and dark skirts were the clothing worn for most day wear within the home.

Next door was a milliner's shop where hats for women, men and children were made and sold. Most popular among the ladies were the wide brimmed straw hats, trimmed with ribbon bands and small flowers. These provided stylish protection from the sun and were perfect to wear while walking in bright daylight.

At dinner one evening Fontine addressed the young women once again.

'Tomorrow you must all wear your new blouses and skirts as our Settlement Committee will meet with each of you. You will be offered several different positions and you can choose the one that suits you best.'

Excitement prevailed the following morning as each young woman waited to be summoned. Clotilde's name was announced first. She approached the door with nervous trepidation.

'Welcome, Clotilde. We are all so pleased to speak with you first.'

'Blandine, it's you, and Father Gilbert too! What a delightful surprise to see you both again.'

'And may I present Madam Fleurier, the wife of our commandant.' Father Gilbert smiled as a beautiful young woman stepped forward to kiss Clotilde on both cheeks and address her.

'Dear Clotilde, there are several different places where you could work here on Grande Terre, but news of your special talent has already reached us from the ship's company. We have heard how well you worked with the children during the long voyage, teaching them reading, writing and numbers. The government school presently has no teacher and all here are hoping that you will choose to become our teacher. But take a moment first to consider this offer, before you reply to us.'

Father Gilbert then explained to Clotilde where she would be living.

'There is a section of Port-de-France that you don't know of as yet. It is located near the outskirts, a sort of village within the wider settlement that encloses the civil, administrative and military establishments. Here our soldiers live in barracks or in small cottages with their families. The judge, solicitors, clerks, medical staff and the Commandant all reside within these precincts. Our large church of Saint Joan is situated here and is used by most of the settlers for Sunday mass, weddings, baptisms and funerals. I am now responsible for the life of the church here in Port-de-France. As well, all of us are able to enjoy our very spacious Government Garden where our families, guests and friends can take the air, free from convicts and the natives. This entire area is fenced and patrolled as our exposed location requires.'

Madam Fleurier spoke next. 'Clotilde, your school is located in the centre of our enclosure in a large wooden cottage. You will have a single classroom containing twelve desks, your teacher's desk and a small supply room. Behind the class room is a sitting room with a small adjoining kitchen and a comfortable bedroom. These are your living quarters. Behind the cottage is a vegetable garden that includes a wooden table and benches, should you choose to enjoy the outdoors. We would expect you to grow some of your own food and maintain the flower garden near the front door. As you will receive a wage for your teaching duties, you can purchase the rest of your food and personal needs from the settlement shops. Everything here lies within a comfortable walking distance.'

'Clotilde, do you have any questions?' asked Father Gilbert.

'No Father Gilbert. You have all given me a good explanation of my work and accommodation.'

'Now we await your final reply.'

'Oh yes, I am so pleased to accept your offer and become your teacher. I will do my very best to make this contribution to Port-de-France.'

And so it was decided. Blandine stepped forward to collect Clotilde and her belongings.

'I'll be taking you to your new home now. We have a cart and horse waiting outside.'

As they filled the cart with Clotilde's belongings she noticed several boxes resting at the back.

'These do not belong to me as I've never seen them before,' Clotilde noted.

'Oh, but they do! Your ship carried supplies for the settlement and among them are items that you may need for the school. Tomorrow we'll unpack them and I'll help you move into the classroom.'

Then overcome with joy, Clotilde and Blandine embraced one another again as they departed, chatting excitedly like two old friends.

After settling Clotilde into her cottage, Blandine left her with a basket of food for the kitchen and a chance to unpack and explore her surroundings.

'I'll be back tomorrow morning with our eldest son, Henri and his friend Jean. The boys are eager to meet their new teacher. Our boys can help us unpack your school supplies and will lift the heavier boxes for us. Rest well and enjoy moving into your new home.'

The cottage was clean and simply furnished and by late afternoon Clotilde had unpacked her personal belongings and spent time in the garden surrounding the school. At the front entrance, two oval flower beds were filled with a variety of blooms. The vegetable garden at the back had been left untended for some time and needed careful weeding and new plantings. 'I'll have to ask Blandine when she comes tomorrow how to go about reclaiming my vegetable garden,' she thought. After a light evening meal of sliced ham, bread and a salad, Clotilde suddenly became very tired. It had been a full and interesting day.

'It is so lovely and quiet here,' she thought. Soon she found herself drifting into a deep and peaceful sleep.

6

Early the next morning Blandine arrived with Henri accompanied by Madame LeBec and her son, Jean. Clotilde felt a warmth begin to grow between the two women and herself.

'Clotilde, Madame LeBec is the judge's wife and patroness of our school. '

'Please call me Vivienne from now on, Clotilde, and always turn to me when you need something new for the school or have any questions. '

'I suggest we all look through the supplies in the store room before we unpack the new boxes,' Blandine called out over her shoulder as the three women set to work.

Clotilde was delighted to find a number of large slates, chalks and wipers available for each student. As she counted them Henri wiped each desk and Jean placed them under the lid. A small round hole was cut into the corner of the desk top and next to it was a groove. 'This is just like our Mater Dei schoolroom,' thought Clotilde. 'There must be inkwells that fit into each hole.' Vivienne brought out boxes of writing materials filled with lined writing paper, penholders, steel nibs and glass inkwells for the teaching of penmanship.

'Clotilde, look at these shelves of books,' Blandine called out.

'I can hardly believe what's here!' Clotilde's excitement grew by the minute as she viewed shelves of reading books, language, spelling and arithmetic study books, and several large maps. There were so many items to help her with her teaching and her interest grew with each discovery. The new supplies included more paper, scissors, pencils, bottles of ink, several hymn books, folksong collections and a large illustrated story book that would be perfect for her to read aloud to the class. Two flat boxes contained pastels, of beautiful hues, together with water colour brushes and paints.

'These will be for your art classes, if you decide to offer them,' remarked Vivienne.

'And now I suggest that we all have lunch,' said Blandine. 'Afterward we'll tell you more about the school program.'

Over fresh fruit, cheese and delicious sweet bread filled with raisins, Vivienne spoke first.

'You will have eleven children ranging from six to twelve years of age - six girls and five boys. Our school day begins at nine o'clock and carries on until eleven thirty when the children go outside to eat their lunches and play. At noon the church bells of Saint Joan will ring the angelus, after which the children take a few minutes to return to the classroom. You will teach until two o'clock when they may leave school for the day. On Wednesday and Saturday, the school will close at noon.'

'I can use the remainder of the afternoons to correct the children's work and prepare for the following day,' Clotilde replied.

'So each Wednesday and Saturday afternoon and Sunday is always free for you to use as you please. Be sure to enjoy our beautiful Government Garden whenever you want and do your shopping as everything is open for business on Saturday afternoon. Every Saturday morning Jean will bring you a sealed envelope from me. It will contain your wages for the week you completed. Clotilde, don't hesitate to call on me if you need to discuss anything that involves the school. I am your patroness and want to help you in every way I can.'

'Thank you both, Vivienne and Blandine, for all you have done for me. I now feel capable of offering your children a strong teaching program. There are so many materials and supplies here and I will lack for nothing.'

'Have you any final questions?'

'Today is Wednesday. Let me set up the classroom during the remainder of this week and on Monday morning I would like to welcome the children to their first day of school. I will be able to teach for four weeks before the Christmas holidays are upon us. '

'We were hoping you would begin soon as the children are looking forward to school once again. We will let all the families know.'

'And before you leave me, I almost forgot to ask you about my very forlorn little vegetable patch behind the cottage. Is there someone who could help me re-establish it?'

Vivienne replied, 'Yes, we have a wonderful gardener, Jacques Vallon, a convict. I will speak to his superiors and I am sure something can be done for you. We will leave you now.'

'Thank you both, and you too, Henri and Jean, for all your kind help.' After bidding them farewell, Clotilde sat at her desk, lost in thought. 'I am so happy that I had the courage to leave Mater Dei and sail to Grande Terre. I feel in my heart that my new life, and Satine's too, will be interesting and full of joy.'

7

'Jacques, you must put your tools away early this afternoon.' Gerard Duphly, the old head gardener of the Port-de-France Government Garden, approached Jacques who was bent over, working on one of the rose beds.

'Madame LeBec, the patroness of our little school, has come to me with a request. We now have a new teacher for the government children and this young woman needs some help with her vegetable garden. '

'Ah, some time ago I looked over the garden at the back of the school house and yes, it's in a very poor state,' Jacques replied.

'You can continue with these roses tomorrow morning. Take a few minutes for your lunch then make your way to the schoolhouse and see what we can do for the new teacher.'

Jacques slowly ate his piece of bread while enjoying a drink of fresh water. From the time he was a young child he had always loved plants. He knew intuitively how to care for them, make then grow tall and strong while planting them in attractive arrangements. After the untimely death of his mother and father, Uncle Leon and Aunt Cecine took him into their home. After his twelfth birthday, Uncle Leon brought Jacques to the Bagatelle Park, to enroll him in its horticultural school. Here he also learned to read and write well, skills that were important for every aspiring gardener. His thoughts roamed back to his life in Paris, three years ago, where at age seventeen he was completing his junior apprenticeship in the Gardens of Napoleon III.

How he loved his work there in the Bagatelle. He and Louis were their two most talented students. When the word had gone out that one of the two of them could be chosen as the head apprentice for the Tuileries Gardens, Jacques heard whisperings that he was the favoured candidate.

'So you hope that you will be chosen for the Tuileries Gardens?' Louis spoke to him with his sneering smile.

'It's up to another to make that choice,' replied Jacques.

'We'll see about that,' Louis smirked and pushed Jacques aside with his shoulder as he passed him.

Later that afternoon when Jacques brought his discarded clippings to the compost heap he noticed four onions on the top of the pile. 'Who would leave good onions like these on a compost heap? They are too fresh to be thrown away,' Jacques thought. 'I'll put them in my pocket and take them home to Aunt Cecine. She can make an onion soup.' Jacques put away his tools and prepared to leave, but when he reached the garden gate two Gendarmes approached him.

'Stop right where you are, young man,' they called out harshly. 'It has been reported to us that you are stealing food from the vegetable garden plots. Don't you know the food grown there is only for the Emperor's household?'

'I have never stolen anything from the garden.'

'We heard that you have something in your pockets. Empty them out, right now.' Jacques removed the four onions and spoke to the gendarmes. 'These were left on the compost heap so I took them. They are not from the Emperor's vegetable garden.'

'We have a witness to the fact that you stole these onions. Your theft was reported to us so you must come with us now. A judge will decide if you are innocent or guilty.'

As Jacques was led away he saw Louis loitering by the gate. 'Farewell, Jacques. It looks like I'll be going to the Tuilleries now instead of you.' So it was Louis who had planned this terrible event. What a fool he had been to take the onions. Overwhelmed by a sudden sense of despair, Jacques realized that this day would be a fateful one that could change his life forever.

Early the following morning Jacques was taken from the cell he had shared the previous night with several men.

'The judge will see you now, and you will receive your sentence.'

As Jacques entered a nearby courtroom, he faced a distinguished looking gentleman, seated behind a table and flanked by armed guards.

'Young man, it has been reported to me that you were an apprentice when you stole four onions from Emperor Napoleon's vegetable garden. You were seen by a witness. Have you anything to say for yourself?'

'Monsieur le Judge, yes, I was an apprentice but I did not steal any onions from a garden. I took them from a waste heap where they had been left.'

Jacques had no way of knowing that weeks earlier this very judge was shown a letter from Grande Terre. Its contents requested that any convicts with horticultural skills be sent urgently to the island, rather than be left in a Parisian prison. There before him stood his chance to assist the new colony.

'In keeping with the law I must now inform you that you will be transported to Grande Terre to complete what should be a sentence of seven years of labour. However, because your offence was a minor one, I will reduce this to four years – one year for each onion that you removed from the garden. A convict ship sails in a few days and you will be aboard it. When your sentence has been completed you may return to France or stay on Grande Terre, where you will be given a parcel of land and your full freedom. Please escort this man away and bring in the next.'

Several mornings later Jacques' Uncle Leon and his weeping Aunt Cecine could only catch a glimpse of him as he boarded the ship, chained to a dozen other men. The seven month voyage was expected to be a hell on earth but Jacques was determined to keep up his spirits and try to stay as healthy as he could. At first he remained chained in a dark space below the deck. After two weeks his group was brought up on deck and his chains were removed. At last he could breathe fresh air and enjoy the sunshine. To his surprise he was placed under guard near the poop deck as other groups were brought up for fresh air. Occasionally another prisoner was unchained and sent to the space where Jacques was being held. When all had been accounted for and returned to the hold, Jacques and three other prisoners were escorted to a different space. This was still below deck but away from the general group of prisoners, closer to an open barred window and in a place to accommodate them standing, if they wished.

The four men spoke together about this change of fortune. Jacques discovered that one of them had studied medicine, another was a civil engineer and the third, a new apprentice accountant. The other three were pleased to learn that Jacques had been a horticultural apprentice at the Bagatelle Gardens. One of them mentioned that they had probably been spared from working the nickel mines as their specialized training could be used in the settlements. There were also opportunities for some exercise above deck and better rations. The voyage was still very difficult but at least it was made bearable by these new arrangements. The time seemed to pass quickly too as the men could converse with each other and support one another during their moments of loneliness and depression.

At last the ship reached Port-de-France and all were allowed to disembark. As each man's name was called, many were directed to a large group of convicts. These men were shackled and led away to work in the mines. When Jacques' name was called, he stepped forward and was met by an elderly man. Together they made their way to a waiting cart.

'I am Gerard Duphly, head gardener of the Government Garden. You will serve your four years as my assistant. There is a small room behind the garden supply shed where you may sleep. If you are hard-working and cooperative, you will be allowed to make full use of your horticultural talents here. Can you do this?' Duphly looked carefully at Jacques. For some reason he immediately liked this tall, thin young man who spoke quietly and looked him straight in the eye when he answered.

'Yes, I am relieved that I was not sent to hard labour in the nickel mines. I will assist you in every way I can.'

'You will be moving among the free settlers and government administrators. You may not socialize with them in any way and must keep your place at all times. I will teach you what I can, but you have come with very high recommendations from the Bagatelle. It's a pity for you that you took the onions, but a blessing for me that you are here in Grande Terre. Work hard and your four years will pass quickly. Who knows, you may even choose to stay on here.'

'I have heard all you have said and I accept your advice. Already I feel the warmth and the open sky of this lovely place beginning to heal my soul. If I can work in a garden I can survive anything.'

Jacques put out his hand and Gerard Duphly took it in his. The two men knew instinctively they could trust one another.

'Enough of this wandering mind,' Jacques said aloud. His lunch was now finished, so he gathered a note book and pencil and made his way to the Government School. 'Let's see what I can do for the new teacher.'

'Mademoiselle, I am the gardener, here to assist you.'

'Please call me Mademoiselle Clotilde. I am looking forward to your help with this poor little garden.'

Jacques paced through the garden making notes as he walked. Moments later he called Clotilde over to join him and soon they were seated at her table.

'You have a lovely old tree in that corner and a space under it for your table and benches. Why not move your table over there, to give you shade during the summer. I have a number of old paving stones and I could make a pathway from your back door to the table. You could work on your garden beds along the pathway and it would also look attractive. I've sketched the locations of different vegetable beds where you can easily grow corn, cabbages, tomatoes, carrots and lettuce. With a framework that I'll make later, peas and climbing beans can add to your food supply. The garden is too small for a potato bed but these can be purchased from the shops. Do you have any suggestions for me?'

Clotilde was surprised at how quickly he worked and how well he could speak, write and draw.

'This would be wonderful just as you have explained it. When can you start work?'

'Monsieur Duphly will give me one full day so perhaps Saturday, the day after tomorrow, would be a suitable time for me to come?'

'Yes, I will be back here in the garden after the children leave school at noon. Thank you for this fine plan.'

On the appointed day Jacques appeared with his garden tools, a wheelbarrow and several boxes of small plants. He began by using a shovel to dig up the garden and turn the soil. When this was finished he took flat paving stones from the wheelbarrow and laid a pathway. The table and benches were relocated with ease. It was now noon and Clotilde noticed how hard he had worked and how much he had accomplished. She carried out a jug of cold water and a covered plate to her table, smiled at Jacques and said, 'You should sit in the shade now and eat this lunch.'

'Thank you, Mademoiselle Clotilde. You are very kind,' replied Jacques. He was amazed when he uncovered the plate to see a chicken drumstick, a large piece of cheese and a small half loaf of bread. It was sweet and filled with raisins. It had been such a long time since he had enjoyed food like this. When lunch was finished he planted the seedlings and asked Clotilde to look over her garden. 'It may rain later this afternoon and these plants will receive a good watering.

In another two weeks I'll bring in some new plants and you can add them to the beds yourself. In this way you will keep your garden always flowering and producing food.'

Jacques could not help but notice Clotilde's blue-green eyes and her beautiful curly chestnut brown hair. She had noted his handsome face, his quietly spoken manner and strong determination to complete the work on her garden.

'I look forward to receiving my next plants. Thank you so much for your hard work today.'

He nodded, packed his tools and returned to the Government Garden.

There he surveyed his handiwork and that of Duphly, as his thoughts travelled back to his arrival on Grande Terre. Nearly two years had passed already and after Christmas he would reach the halfway mark of his sentence. The time had slipped away quickly and he had achieved much toward developing the garden. In his very first week Gerard presented him with a problem.

'Jacques, what can I do with this large piece of open land, to make it more pleasing to the people here? I was thinking of hedgerows enclosing garden beds set out in a geometrical design. What are your thoughts?'

'Monsieur Duphly, do we really want to copy the formal French gardening style with its fountains, cascades and evergreens clipped to perfection? Or do you favour the Dutch influence with William of Orange's topiary, cones and pyramids. We'll both be worked to death cutting and clipping if we choose either of these styles!'

'What ideas do you have instead of these?'

'In my last months at the Bagatelle I saw a painting of an English garden planned in a completely new way. This garden was less formal, with trees being allowed to grow into their natural shapes. The pathways flowed freely to take advantage of different views. Bright flowers were mass-planted in garden beds that had been set out in scrolls and ovals. The whole effect was natural and uncluttered and was designed by a landscaper with the strange name of Capability Brown. Perhaps some of these ideas could be introduced into the Government Garden here?'

Excitedly Gerard remarked. 'May I suggest that we divide the garden into four grand spaces with winding pathways all converging into the centre. A three-tiered fountain will provide the focus of attention there. You could carry out your tree plantings and establish garden beds shaped as you see fit. You have developed this flair for landscape gardening from your years at the Bagatelle and you also see the big overall picture. Let me always check your plans progressively to evaluate them and we will both set to work.'

Slowly the Government Garden grew into a beautiful open space where all who used it could enjoy its relaxed ambience. Everyone seemed delighted with the special garden beds blazing in their riot of colours and scents. Tall trees provided shade where cast iron garden benches invited restful contemplation and provided opportunity for intimate conversation. Lovers met in these spaces, groups strolled and exchanged greetings. The children were not forgotten either and in a special section just for them, Jacques built a *follie*. This folly included a labyrinth of shoulder-high clipped hedges where the children could run, get lost and hide from one other. Nearby two swings and a see-saw provided more play space.

At the garden's centre where all the pathways converged, a magnificent three-tiered fountain was erected in a large reflecting pool. Around its perimeter, flower beds added colour and drama to the setting. As the garden slowly reached its glory, Jacque's first two years had proved to be interesting and filled with happiness. Perhaps it was a good thing after all to have collected those four onions!

8

The next year passed quickly as Clotilde's hard work established her little school. Its doors opened officially in mid-January when eleven young students came forward to greet her, their eyes shining with excitement. Between teaching, maintaining her vegetable garden, shopping on Saturday afternoons and spending time on Sunday visiting with friends, her days were filled. Yvonne, another young settler who arrived in March, was only too happy to offer a weekly singing class to the school children.

As July approached, the colony received an exciting piece of news that brought a special sense of jubilation to all. Vivienne was the first to alert the school to this event.

'Clotilde, I have great news to share with you, which you must also pass on to the children. As patroness of this school it's my pleasure to let you know that our Settlement, Port-de-France, is going to be officially renamed on a community day, scheduled in October of this year.'

'Why are we calling Port-de-France by another name?' Clotilde asked.

'In letter from the Emperor, it seems that Port-de-France is often being confused with Fort-de-France in Martinique. As our French colonial presence is expanding throughout the world, it has been deemed necessary to identify our settlement here a by a new name, that of Noumea. To mark this event Governor Gillian and Father Pierre Rougeyron, our Vicar Apostolic, will leave Tahiti and sail to Grande Terre where they will both officially inaugurate the change. The Emperor anticipates that this colony will continue to grow very quickly during the next few years and it is possible that Governor Gillian may eventually live here among us. '

'This should be a grand occasion and I hope that the children and I can participate in the festivities.'

'We plan to organize a tour of our settlement and this will include the Government School. Perhaps the children can display some of their school work and even prepare a short program to welcome these distinguished guests.'

'Rest assured, Vivienne, that we will begin our preparations immediately,' Clotilde replied.

On the following Sunday, an excited Satine met Clotilde in the Government Garden. 'Have you heard the news about the renaming celebrations?'

'Oh yes, Vivienne told me all about it and I will feature the school and the children in this event. The official party will visit us during the tour.'

Satine continued, 'Anne Fleurier will be the hostess for a gala dinner in her home that will include: Governor Gillian, Father Rougeyron, Father Gilbert, two French officers accompanying the visitors, Judge LeBec and his wife Vivienne, Anne and Commandant Fleurier. The Governor will be staying in the guest rooms at the Commandant's large cottage. Father Rougeyron will reside with Father Gilbert in his cottage next to the church. But best of all, Anne has asked me to play and sing for the guests after the dinner. I am very excited and have already selected my program and started to practice.'

'Oh Satine, you will add such a tone to this occasion.'

'There will also be a special mass of celebration so I'll play the organ on this day as well. For my performance after the dinner, Anne has offered me one of her ball gowns and a pearl necklace so that I can present myself at my best. Her maid will also arrange my hair. I'm so excited at the prospect of this wonderful day!'

The girls chatted on and after returning to her cottage Clotilde looked through her clothing. Her wardrobe really needed something new and appropriate. 'I have a pair of good shoes,' she thought to herself, 'but a white blouse and black skirt seems too plain for my day wear. I'll visit the LeBlanc sisters next Saturday and have something made up for the occasion.'

Saturday finally arrived and an excited Clotilde entered the dress shop. 'You've come to see us, Clotilde, about something new for the day of renaming celebrations. We are both being run off our feet with orders for new dresses but we will also accommodate your wishes. Everyone must look their best on that day.'

'Madame LeBlanc, the official party will visit our school as part of the tour and I'm preparing a program for the children to present. I need something more appropriate for classroom wear on that day.'

'Ah, it should be a blouse and skirt, but it need not be black and white. Just look at this lovely navy blue skirt fabric. It is a most attractive colour yet is still sturdy, suitable and long wearing. With your chestnut hair and blue green eyes, what do you think of this cotton muslin that just arrived?' Madame LeBlanc spread out a roll of soft cotton fabric on her large table. It had thin alternating pin stripes of dark blue and deep brown on a pale green background.

'Oh, I love the pattern and its colours! This would make such a beautiful blouse and it works so well with the skirt fabric,' Clotilde replied.

'I'll keep the stripes in the blouse vertical while introducing a trim of the same fabric cut on the bias. This trim will be used for a small high buttoned collar and high buttoned cuffs on its long tapered sleeves. All the buttons will be self covered in bias. There should be a few tucks running straight down the front to complete the look. These will set off the pin stripes. Now let me place the skirt material next to it. *Voila*, isn't this stylish, yet practical? '

'It will be just perfect for the occasion.'

Throwing her arms around Clotilde she exclaimed, '*Oui*, I am a true genius when it comes to fashion. Is it not so? You will be stunning in this outfit. Wear it on Sundays too after the celebrations, when you and your pretty little friend, the musician, walk together in the garden. I see that tall, young gardener look admiringly at you as you walk by. What will he make of you then?' Laughing she told Clotilde, 'Oh yes, I see and know everything that goes on here in Grande Terre.'

'Oh, Madame LeBlanc,' replied Clotilde who was now blushing. 'You are indeed a genius and thankfully you also have my measurements. Please make this up for me when you have the time. I look forward to wearing it.' But as Clotilde returned home she mused to herself. Whatever could Madame have meant when she spoke of Jacques, looking at her?

* * *

At last, the day for the renaming celebration arrived. The entire settlement was filled with excitement. Boxes of flowers were planted along the two main streets. The paving had been swept clean and several of the shop fronts were repainted. The celebrations started with a solemn mass, celebrated by the Vicar Apostolic and Father Gilbert. It was here that the renaming of Noumea was formally announced to cheers and clapping. Afterward the official party enjoyed a morning tea in the Government Garden, looking its most beautiful for the occasion. Then the tour began and shortly before lunch the group of dignitaries entered the school. The children rose in unison and spoke as one.

'*Bon Jour*, Good Day. We welcome you to our school.' Then they sang a song of greeting and a French folk song. Clotilde was introduced together with Yvonne. Samples of school work had been displayed throughout the room and this was examined by the Governor and Apostolic Vicar.

'What fine, careful work we see here. Well done, children and to your teachers, Mademoiselles Clotilde and Yvonne.' Clotilde accepted their praise with her usual charm. Then as a special treat, the governor excused all the children from school immediately after their lunch. Amidst loud cheers they were set free to enjoy the remainder of the day as they wished.

During the evening, Anne and Commandant Fleurier hosted their gala dinner party. Anne looked her most beautiful in a lavish ball gown, with diamonds at her throat and ears; the gems sparkling in the candlelight. The food had been specially prepared by their French chef and the best wine served for the occasion. Afterward when all met in the drawing room for coffee, sherry and cognac, Satine approached the piano. She was dressed in a green silk ball gown offset by a double strand pearl necklace, her blonde hair elegantly coiffed.

Her singing and playing thrilled the audience and at the conclusion of her performance, the governor stood to formally thank her for, '... the finest singing I have heard in this part of the world.'

Afterward Satine appeared in the kitchen where a plate of the same food served to the guests was offered to her. As she ate at the cook's great table, the kitchen helpers all thanked her. Anne had allowed them to listen to her performance, from behind the double doors. Later a maid helped Satine unhook her dress and prepare for bed. Before the candles were blown out for the night, Anne appeared in Satine's room. She embraced and kissed her, thanking her for the part she played in making the dinner a great success.

'Oh Satine, this is what I am made for, not only to be a wife and mother to our children but to be an outstanding hostess. In years to come the Commandant and I will entertain many dignitaries from many countries. This is my true life's purpose and I have begun to fulfill it tonight.'

'And thank you, Anne, for providing me with your beautiful dress and pearls. This has truly been the happiest day of my life too. And to think we now live in Noumea on Nouvelle-Caledonie. What a day this has been!'

9

Clotilde's school year of 1867 began with the arrival of three new children as more ships reached Noumea carrying settlers and supplies. Two of her eldest students left the Government School bound for France and the homes of relatives. Here they would complete the remaining years of their upper school education before returning home to Noumea once again. With their loss and the addition of one extra desk, Clotilde was happy to accommodate the newcomers. One day after school was dismissed, she and Blandine sorted through a box of new school supplies. Again her eyes fell upon two more large boxes of pastels. Their colours were breathtaking and included every hue under the sun.

'Blandine, if only I knew what to do with these beautiful art supplies, I would offer art lessons to a small group of students. Have you ever worked with pastels before?'

'No, I never have, but I've often wished that I could study art. Yet I seem to remember that Henriette Maison, the wife of an officer, has a great ability in the field of botanical art. Her flower drawings and paintings are so well done that she sends them to the National Horticultural Society in Paris. The staff members there are very interested in documenting the flora of France's many colonies.'

'Would you approach her to see if she would teach us how to draw flowering plants and to use these pastels to colour them?'

'Yes, I'll visit her when I finish helping you here. Wouldn't it be wonderful if she would accept the two of us as her students?'

'If she agrees, I will offer her a set of new watercolour paints and two brushes. We have extra ones here that I may never use.'

Several days later Blandine returned with good news. 'Henriette will be happy to give us six lessons and will offer these at the school on a Wednesday afternoon, after the students leave.'

And so the two young women enthusiastically began their study of floral botanical art. They first learned how to draw in pencil and then to apply the colours. Next they blended these with a small square of chamois to create a picture with depth. They practiced setting out the seed pods, the young plants with their exposed roots, then crowning the collection with a mature flowering plant and its bud together on a single stem. These items were arranged on the paper in various compositions. Clotilde's front garden provided them with specimens for their study. When the lessons had finished and Clotilde felt experienced enough, she offered floral botanical drawing to her class. Three of the older girls were eager to begin and soon Wednesday afternoon classes became their new focus.

As the weather grew cooler, plants with different colours were needed so Clotilde and the three girls packed their pencils, pastels and sketching boards and moved to the Government Garden. Here they could work out of doors in the afternoon sunlight. They found benches to sit on near some of the more unusual flower beds. Occasionally people on their daily walks would stop to smile and chat, admiring their artistic efforts. One afternoon Jacques presented Clotilde with a beautiful plant, resplendent with colourful foliage. It was crowned with a deep golden canna lily. He placed it on the ground before her, smiled and then moved quickly away. When it rained during the next week a visit to the garden became impossible. To her surprise, a glass jar filled with a bouquet of vividly coloured flowers appeared on her back table. She knew who had brought it and felt gratitude for this thoughtful gesture. She left the empty jar on her table with a thank you note slipped underneath it. The next day the jar and note were both gone.

* * *

Three weeks had passed and Clotilde spoke to Yvonne with some consternation.

'Satine must be very busy. So much time has passed since I last spoke with her. Have you heard any news that might explain why she hasn't contacted either of us?' Walking with Yvonne in the garden the following Sunday afternoon, she finally caught a glimpse of Satine, strolling ahead on the arm of a young man. He was dressed in the uniform of a French military officer. As soon as Satine noticed Clotilde, she and her partner hurried over to greet them.

'Clotilde and Yvonne, I'd like you to meet Germond. He arrived here in Nouvelle-Caledonie for the renaming day, as part of a military escort for the Vicar Apostolic and the Governor.'

'I'm delighted to meet you both,' he replied in a resonant voice. 'Satine has spoken often of you. We met after she played and sang for us so beautifully at the Commandant's dinner and it has been my pleasure to spend Sunday afternoons with her since then.'

'And it is my pleasure to meet you, Germond.' Clotilde couldn't help but notice how radiant and happy Satine looked and she felt a deep sense of joy for her friend. Perhaps Satine had found someone to love and care for her.

'Later this year Germond will be recalled to the main administration centre in Tahiti. I know this seems very sudden, but he has asked me to go away with him when he leaves. When his orders are finalized, I will request that Anne Fleurier and the Commandant allow me to leave their service. Germond and I will be married before we depart for Tahiti. Oh Clotilde, I can hardly believe that I will be leaving Nouvelle-Caledonie before Christmas! I have been waiting for an opportunity to tell you this news and today it has finally happened.'

'Congratulations, Satine and Germond. I wish you both much happiness. Please come and visit me before you finally leave. Father Gilbert will miss your organ playing so much.'

Germond replied, 'There are many ships carrying settlers that will arrive here during the next few years, Clotilde. Noumea will grow larger and another musician will surely be among the new arrivals.'

Saying their farewells the two groups went their separate ways, but before the day was finished Clotilde experienced yet another surprise. When she reached her home, a letter from Mater Dei had been slipped under the front door. Tearing open the letter Clotilde noticed that the handwriting was not that of Sister Celeste, but belonged instead to Mother Germain. Why did she feel this sudden sense of dread? Sitting down at her schoolroom desk she closed her eyes for a moment before she began to read its contents.

Our dear Clotilde,

Over the past several years we have enjoyed receiving your letters and learning about the life you are experiencing on the other side of the world. All of us here at Mater Dei are very proud of your achievements, both as a teacher in the Government School and in the way you are living out your days as a fine young woman. Unfortunately this letter contains a piece of news that will bring sadness to your heart.

I know how close you were to Sister Celeste and how eagerly she awaited your letters. As soon as she heard from you she always wrote back immediately and made a great effort to read your messages to all the sisters during their evening meals. She loved you in a special way and always kept you in her prayers and thoughts.

Several weeks ago a dreadful sickness spread through Paris and Sister Celeste became very ill with a high fever. We nursed her and prayed continually. Three days later as her fever increased, our dear Celeste died a peaceful death. On the night before she left us she whispered this message.

'Tell my dearest Clotilde that I will always love her and will keep watch over her in the years ahead.' And so dear heart, we all send you our loving comfort and sympathy. Please keep your letters coming to us as we never forget 'our girls.'

With our love and prayers,

Mother Germain

One cannot describe the feeling of loss that washed over Clotilde as she read these words. Tears of pain began to flow. Not only would she lose the closeness of

Satine's presence but her only other experience of being loved was taken from her now, through the death of Sister Celeste. The terrible sense of abandonment she had first experienced as a tiny child, brought to the Mater Dei Orphanage, almost smothered her once again. She cried through the night until a deep sleep finally settled over her.

On the following morning, the radiant sunshine and the music of singing birds brought Clotilde a new sense of hope and purpose. She awoke with the feeling of a loving presence surrounding her. 'Sister Celeste, you are with me,' she whispered to herself. 'I can sense your loving presence. You will watch over me and all will be well. My life here in Noumea will be filled with happiness and blessings.'

10

Satine was a radiant, beautiful bride. She and Germond were married on a glorious morning in the Church of Saint Joan. Clotilde and Yvonne were among many guests. These also included Commandant Fleurier and Anne, Judge LeBec and Vivienne, together with a number of military personnel. At the conclusion of the ceremony, six officers in full dress uniform formed a guard of honour as Satine and Germond walked under the archway formed by two lines of crossed swords. An afternoon tea was provided in the private garden of the commandant's house. Adjoining it was a small, well-furnished cottage where Satine and Germond would stay until their ship left for Tahiti two days later.

Before the wedding, Clotilde was invited to visit Satine in her room. They enjoyed a long final visit together and shared many memories of their lives, from their days at Mater Dei until the present.

'Come and look at my wedding gown,' Satine called out as she led Clotilde to her adjoining small sitting room. 'You are the first to see it.' Draped over a chair was an exquisite dress and veil.

'Oh, it's absolutely beautiful,' Clotilde remarked. 'Where did you find all that white satin and the long lace veil? I thought you would be wearing the gown and veil from your trousseau?'

'Anne wanted me to look more stylish since so many of the guests were connected to the Comandant's military personnel. I didn't feel that I could disagree with her as she has shown me such kindness. As you may have guessed, Madame LeBlanc designed and made the dress. It is my wedding present from Anne and the Commandant.'

'How kind of them both, Satine. They must think so highly of you. But what will become of Empress Eugenie's dress and veil?' asked Clotilde.

'Ah, one of the maids in Anne's household has requested leave to marry. She didn't have a suitable wedding dress and veil so I offered my ensemble from the trousseau to her. It fit her perfectly and she looked lovely in the outfit. Annette was beside herself with joy. I did find a way to make another happy with the gift from the Empress, so all has ended well.'

Satine would always be her dearly-loved friend, but of late she had also become a very grand lady. 'I hope so much that Satine and Germond will find happiness together in Tahiti,' Clotilde thought. Days later as their ship sailed away from Noumea, she watched from the shore until it was only a speck on the horizon.

On returning to her cottage, she discovered a note from Vivienne, asking if she could speak with her on Friday afternoon. 'We have already planned our final Christmas presentation for the parents of the school children, so it must be an important event she wants to discuss with me.' On Friday, Vivienne appeared and asked Clotilde to sit with her in the empty school room.

'You may have noticed that there are many ships arriving with new settlers. Noumea is going to become a large village next year, instead of a small settlement. As more children arrive we will need places in the school for them. Already you have squeezed a child into every possible space in your classroom and next year I will have four more children for you to teach.'

'Vivienne, I don't know where I'll be able to put them. We are already so crowded. Is there a chance that the little ones can receive special teaching from another place?'

'We will try to accommodate this as you should now be teaching only eight to twelve year old pupils, before they leave to continue their education in France. When you open the school next January in 1868, I have been asked to tell you that this will be the final year the Government School will be operating. Already there is a large School of Saint Joan being planned and a group of teaching nuns from Paris will be sailing here next year to staff the school. The building of the new school will commence in March.'

'I am not surprised as Noumea needs many new services. Already the settlement has accepted a hundred new settlers and homes must also be built for them and their families,' Clotilde replied, with a sense of disquiet.

'We are also expecting another doctor and a small hospital to be built soon. More shops have required a third paved street, so we are growing quickly, and Emperor Napoleon III is greatly pleased at this. As you may have guessed, the cottage you are now living in must be expanded as more government residences are needed. There will be time next year to find another good living place for you and further teaching opportunities, if you wish.'

'Thank you for giving me this information, Vivienne. It gives me a chance now to think about future plans I may want to make. Yes, life in Noumea is beginning to change very quickly.'

The school year finished on a high note as Clotilde's Christmas holidays came upon her. She had organized another closing program, attended by all her student's enthusiastic parents. Each of the children was featured in some small way and the group singing and poetry recitations were all well presented. Collecting a portion of extra money she had saved from her wages, Clotilde decided to treat herself to a new dress and hat to wear on Christmas Day. Off she went again to Madame LeBlanc, who as usual had new samples of light floral muslin on display.

'Let me suggest several patterns that would suit your hair and eyes, Clotilde. I have this elegant floral toile pattern of pastel flowers scattered on a pale turquoise background. I'll trim it with some wide lace at the edges of your softly puffed sleeves and make a collar of lace for the bodice.'

'I love the design and colour of this fabric. It will do beautifully.'

'See this gorgeous turquoise velvet ribbon? Let me make a sash from it and I'll craft three small bows to decorate the dress front. When you buy your hat, bring it to me and I'll trim it with the same velvet band and a bow. You will be so beautiful for Christmas, my little darling! Oh, how I enjoy making women look their best!'

'Thank you, Madame LeBlanc. You can always be counted on to bring out our best,' Clotilde responded. Walking home with a spring in her step, Clotilde whispered aloud, 'There's nothing like a new outfit to raise one's spirits.'

* * *

And with the approach of Christmas, there was another one who also looked forward with great expectancy to this date. The time had finally arrived for Jacques to complete his four year sentence and be awarded with a full pardon. He had worked very hard during the past four years and carefully observed all the conditions that had been placed upon him. Duphly, the head gardener was pleased with his work and could be counted on to offer a good word on his behalf. Finally the long awaited letter arrived, requesting his presence at the Commandant's office the following afternoon. He showed the letter to Duphly, who placed his arms around Jacques and wished him success. Jacques washed his best shirt, hands and face, combed his hair and set off the following day.

'Please step forward, young man. Are you the one called Jacques Vallon?'

'I am he, Sir.'

'Are you aware that you have now completed your sentence? I have been told that you have faithfully kept all your terms of service.'

'Yes, I have.'

'I have received much praise on your behalf from your superiors and I wish to commend you on the work you have achieved in the Government Garden. Through your efforts and those of Duphly, we have one of the finest gardens here in the South Pacific. As of now, you are a free man and so you have a choice - either to return to France or to stay on here to continue your fine work. Should you decide to remain with us you will be rewarded with a parcel of land in Noumea and the opportunity to pursue paid work. You could have a great future here, but your choice will be honoured of course. Now, I await your reply, Monsieur Vallon?'

'He called me Monsieur,' thought Jacques. 'At last, I am truly free.'

'I have considered your generous offer, Sir, and I wish to remain in Nouvelle-Caledonie. There are many opportunities here and my skills could be useful in Noumea. I am also happy to be living with the people of Noumea as they have always treated me with kindness.'

'Well done, young man. Now step over to the table and sign your pardon before my notary. Here is a note from me as well, to present to the men's clothing store. As my gift to you, please choose a new pair of boots, two new shirts and one pair of trousers to assist you in your new life. There is also a small packet of money here on the table to help you until you are paid by the Government Garden. Duphly is growing old so he still requires your assistance. You can continue to live in the garden shed until you take possession of your land and begin to build your own home. Enjoy and respect your freedom and you will create a fine life for yourself here with us.'

As the Commandant rose, he opened his arms, formally embraced Jacques then cried out, 'To the Glory of France!'

Jacques replied, 'To the Glory of France! And thank you, Sir, for your generosity. I will never disappoint you.'

He signed his paper with a flourish. As waves of joy engulfed him, Jacques made his way toward the clothing shop. For the first time in many years he was filled with joy. He even wanted to sing. Jacques began to run and then to jump - free, free at last! Finally he could write to Uncle Leon and Aunt Cecine, telling them he was alive and well, with an opportunity to create a good life here. Just the thought of casting off his shabby clothing, to enjoy fresh meat, cheese and fruit again, to determine his future and earn some money, to fall in love and even to marry - all these wonderful possibilities put a great spring in his step.

'I am a free man now named Monsieur Jacques Vallon!' he shouted to the heavens. 'Noumea has become my new home.'

11

Christmas Mass was particularly beautiful that year. The church was filled with fresh flowers, another organist had been found and the weather was sunny. Clotilde walked to the church dressed in her attractive new outfit, as she exchanged greetings with everyone she met along the way. At the end of the service she was startled to see Jacques seated among the congregation. He looked so handsome in a new shirt, trousers and boots. His hair had been trimmed, instead of being tied back with a cord. He saw her and smiled as he moved toward her, confident and assured.

'*Joyeux Noel,*' he greeted her.

'Jacques, you have received your pardon,' she blurted out.

'Indeed I have. You are looking at a free man now and one who wishes to walk with you as you return to your home. May I have this honour?'

'Yes, you may.' Yet as they left together, she suddenly became worried. Would the people of Noumea, all her pupils and their parents, accept her and Jacques walking together? To her great relief, everyone smiled and greeted them as they made their way out of the church grounds. Others pressed toward Jacques, expressing their happiness at seeing him move freely among them. Many greeted Clotilde and wished her a *Joyeux Noel.* Two of her smallest pupils approached to admire the lovely dress and touch the lace on her sleeves.

As she and Jacques moved away he suggested they make a tour of the Government Garden, as the day was such a fine one. She was delighted to accompany him as he pointed out several features she hadn't noticed before. He also showed her the new flowers he had planted especially for Christmas.

'These were sent to me on the ship that carried Satine and Germond back to Tahiti. They are flowers that have never been seen here on Nouvelle-Caledonie before.'

'Oh, they are so large and colourful. I would love to make a drawing of each of them.'

As the afternoon passed Clotilde suddenly felt very hungry. 'Jacques, I need something to eat and you must be starving. I have cooked a small ham and would be very happy to have you join me for a late afternoon Christmas dinner.'

Returning to her cottage, he helped her set the outdoor table as she brought out bread, cheese, sliced ham and a salad. The meal was also celebrated with a small bottle of red wine. As they shared her delicious Christmas fare together, they talked on and on. Somehow it felt so easy to speak about the many things they had never told anyone before. Each felt the presence of a friend in the other – one who would totally understand and never judge harshly. Jacques unburdened himself first.

'I have always wanted you to know the true story behind my conviction, Clotilde.' He told her of his happiness with his family and his aunt and uncle, who helped him all through his apprenticeship at the Bagatelle. Then he shared the incident about the four onions, his four year sentence and the wonderful opportunities he had experienced working with old Duphly in the Government Garden. She wept when she learned he had suffered for a crime he never committed, enduring it all with courage.

'I was a tiny child of two years when someone brought me to the Mater Dei Orphanage in Paris and then left me there. Again and again I waited for someone to take me back home, but no one ever came.' She told him about Sister Celeste, the one person who had loved her like a mother and how her death a few months before had left her devastated. She was grateful to the sisters and Mother Germain, who gave her the skills to read and write and find the strength to become a teacher.

As they spoke of their joys and sufferings, their two hearts opened to one another. A deep connection began to grow as the roots of their being slowly entwined. They drew closer together on the bench. Jacques longed to cherish and protect her. Clotilde longed to console him for the pain he had endured and support the talents he shared so generously. Their hands brushed tentatively. Then at last they held each other, quietly and tenderly, her head resting on his heart, until a multitude of stars appeared above them in the infinite shining heavens.

12

The Christmas holiday period passed quickly as Clotilde prepared for the final year she would be teaching in the Government School. She and Jacques spent more of their time together and he joined her most evenings for dinner, before returning to the place he still occupied in the garden shed. 'I'm living there for the present to save money for a surprise I'll be sharing with you very soon.'

'Can't you give me even a little hint of what it is?' Clotilde replied.

'I can tell you this much. Duphly wishes to retire from full time work and he has offered me the paid position of chief gardener of the Government Garden. I agreed immediately, as I can carry on the work I've begun there and that I enjoy so much.'

'Oh Jacques, that is a wonderful surprise!'

'Oh, but that is not the big surprise I've planned to show you! You must wait a little longer to discover that secret. Did I tell you that there are two young men who have also requested to serve their apprenticeships with me?'

'What good news. Now you will have helpers to work with you as the garden takes so much of your time during the summer.'

Finally the day for the opening of school arrived and Clotilde welcomed her students into a very crowded classroom. It was good to be teaching again, working with these lovely children. 'I only wonder what I will be doing when next year arrives,' she thought to herself.

On Friday after the last child had left the school, Jacques surprised her at the front door.

'Clotilde, can you spend the next hour or two with me? The time has come to show you my surprise.'

'At last, Jacques, let's be off before I die of curiosity!'

Together they walked to a large section of unoccupied land a short distance from the Government Garden. It was protected by the perimeter fence and was home to several beautiful old shade trees.

'Within this corner where you see a marking on the ground I made with a spade, is a large and beautiful piece of land. It now belongs to me. Here I will build a house and develop a garden. It was granted to me by Commandant Fleurier after I chose to stay on in Noumea.'

'How wonderful! You now own a piece of land.'

'Come over to this corner and look at the place where the house will be standing. I have already found several men who will start to build it in the next week. They wish to begin work now, as their skills will be required in late April for the School of Saint Joan. We have already drawn up the plans.'

Jacques unrolled a large paper and placed the drawing in Clotilde's hands. 'You can see from this plan where the different rooms will be positioned. Walk with me as I show the house to you.'

'You've planned your house already. I am so excited at what you have achieved.'

'This is the space for the front veranda and entrance. Right here outside the veranda I'll plant two large flower beds, filled with bright colours. There will be a sitting room and dining room right here, next is a wash room, then three bedrooms branch out from a hallway. Finally the semi-detached kitchen is located at the back and the privy lies over there.' Taking her hand he drew her forward.

'Come along, for just outside where I stand now, will be a large covered veranda where another table and chairs can accommodate friends and become a second working space.'

'And where will your garden be?'

'The kitchen and vegetable garden will lie in the corner over here, to capture the sun during the entire day. And in this furthest corner I will build a shed, at some future time, to house the seed bank collection that I am planning. There is such interest in the flora and foliage of this new colony that I'm setting up a program in which I will offer botanical materials to the National Horticultural Society in Paris. I hope one day to import new plants from the surrounding islands as well and prepare these for future collections in France. My work is well cut out for me now. What do you think of all this, Clotilde?'

'I'm completely speechless. What a wonderful future you have planned for yourself.'

'This is not only for me, but for the two of us. I have something important I want to ask you and now the time has come.' He cleared his throat then began to speak slowly, never taking his eyes off her. 'Clotilde, I'm asking you to marry me. I love you alone and have loved you since the first day I met you, in the school garden. Make me the happiest man alive by saying, yes, to me.'

Clotilde was shocked and delighted as she felt waves of joy flood over her. 'He loves me', she thought. 'And I love him too.'

'Oh, Jacques, yes, my answer is yes. I love you so much. Yes, I will marry you.'

With that he swept her into the air and whirled her around. Then bringing her back to earth again he took her gently into his arms and kissed her, again and again. When they finally caught their breath and faced one another a loud cheering and clapping was heard. Behind them the builders had arrived unnoticed and were celebrating with both of them.

'Congratulations to you both,' they cried out.

Jacques laughingly replied, 'Now everyone on Nouvelle-Caledonie will know the news about us, Clotilde,' and he kissed her again. And so it was decided then and there. They would marry and build their life together, here on this beautiful piece of land in Noumea.

* * *

The following months disappeared in a blur of activity. In early February, Clotilde and Jacques spoke with Father Gilbert and asked him to marry them. Together they selected the date for their wedding. As Easter arrived on the 12th of April in 1868, their wedding date was set for the first Saturday after Easter Sunday. Once that was settled, the business of house building and furnishing was uppermost in both their minds. Every Saturday afternoon Clotilde and Jacques walked to their land to inspect the progress of their new home. First the wooden flooring was laid, sanded, sealed and then the framing of the house began. There was an abundance of timber nearby and two sawmills had now begun working, so a constant flow of timber was always available. By the end of February the shingled roof was finished, the walls were up and the exterior timber cladding had begun. Soon the windows were framed and glass windows hung and in mid-March the inner walls and doors were nearly completed.

'At the rate the men are working our house will be finished about three weeks before we are married', Jacques told her excitedly. 'Next Saturday we can both walk through our new home for the first time.'

'I can hardly wait to actually move through the different rooms and begin to plan what we will need to get started,' Clotilde replied. 'We should have our kitchen and dining room furnished as well as our bedroom. The rest can wait until later and be set up bit by bit. There is so much I will have to do, as well as teach. '

'I agree with you. As we will be living in our own home by then only the essentials should be ready for us. You will be leaving your room behind the school and I'll finally say farewell to my cramped garden shed.'

'Vivienne has told me that we may still take vegetables from the garden behind the school until our own garden can feed us. Everything should work out very well for us, but we won't have a minute to spare.'

A large warehouse and storage space had been built at the end of Noumea's third business street during the previous year. Many household items brought over on the supply ships found their way there. Settlers could purchase home wares: bedding, crockery, cutlery and cooking items to set up housekeeping. These were available on credit for families beginning their lives in Noumea. Jacques' wages were spent on paying the builders and purchasing building materials. Clotilde's wages were used to buy a new bed, a dresser, a large table and four chairs. Her kitchen goods and furnishings were bought on credit, to be paid for over time. Jacques bought himself a new suit and shirt to wear for the wedding while Clotilde had her beautiful wedding dress and veil safely stored in the trousseau.

At last the house was finished. They hired a horse cart and together collected the furnishings for their home. Two of the builders offered an hour of their free time to help Jacques transport the heavy items. Blandine presented the couple with a large braided rug she and several women had made. This would be placed in the sitting room. A smaller rug found a space next to the bed. Piece by piece their furniture was carried into the new home and set in place under Clotilde's direction. Several kerosene lamps and candles were brought out for their use at night. She and Yvonne packed dishes and cutlery into a large kitchen cupboard, together with a few cooking pots and utensils. Lastly the bed was made and the dresser with six large drawers and a framed mirror completed their bedroom furnishings. Across a corner, a pole was placed for their hanging space and a low shelf below this held their shoes. Finally the new house was ready for Clotilde and Jacques to occupy after the wedding. Both of them could catch their breath now and attend to their everyday work.

13

'Clotilde, Have you a minute to spend with me?'

'Come in. What can I do for you, Henriette?'

'First let me congratulate you on your coming wedding. Madame LeBlanc told me this wonderful news and everyone is so happy for you both. I've just spoken with Vivienne who mentioned that this Government School will be closing at the end of the year. I asked her if there were any sets of watercolours available and if so, could I have one. She was in agreement.'

'I have several of these just sitting in the storeroom because I don't use them with my botanical art classes. I can even give you two sets if you'd like, with an extra brush for each.'

'I'm really grateful for this and in exchange I'd like to offer you two more lessons. I will meet you on Wednesdays after school.'

'Henriette, have you time now to take a quick look at these two drawings. I feel confident about layering and blending several colours. '

'Clotilde, these are beautiful! You have become so skilful at working with soft pastels. One day you could become a genuine botanical illustrator.'

'There is one final technique I need to acquire. I can't use a pastel to add a detail or do fine shading, as the line is too coarse. '

'What you want for fine work is a hard pastel pencil. You can sharpen this and get a very delicate line that can be left as it is, or blended in. I have a number of these pencils in brown, dark green and a deep rust red colour. You can have two of each in exchange for the painting sets. Never use black as it creates too high a contrast. Brown is more subtle.'

'I'll take up your offer of two classes as I may have an occasion to use my botanical drawing skills with Jacques' future work. We'll visit the store room now to collect your watercolour sets and brushes. Near the end of the year many items will have to be moved to the new School of Saint Joan. I've been told to take another full box of pastels and a good supply of drawing paper for myself and I plan to do just that. Oh, Henriette, my life will change completely after this year is over. I'm looking forward so much to my marriage and to a happy future with Jacques.'

'You will both have a wonderful life together,' Henriette replied, putting her arms around Clotilde.

At last, Easter Sunday arrived. During the week before the wedding, Clotilde was free from teaching as all school children celebrated an Easter holiday. They would not be returning again for two full weeks. She and Yvonne put the final touches to the new home, bringing in food supplies and their clothing. All was in readiness for the newlyweds.

The nuptial mass would be celebrated on Saturday morning. All the invitations had been sent and Clotilde envisaged a very full church. On Friday afternoon she took her wedding dress and veil out of the trousseau, shook out a few wrinkles and hung the dress on a satin padded hanger. This, together with a small bottle of scented hair wash, was a surprise gift from Madame LeBlanc. She filled a bath and washed her hair, drying it in the sun and brushing it until it shone. Tomorrow morning Blandine and Yvonne would arrive to dress her hair and help her into her gown and veil. All three of them would walk to the church where Jacques would meet her at the church door and present her with the wedding bouquet. He wanted to arrange this himself and would select only the most beautiful seasonal flowers. She knew she wouldn't sleep well tonight as her excitement grew by the minute.

A morning filled with sunlight greeted Clotilde as she awoke. Today would be her wedding day. After a light breakfast, her last meal in this little cottage, she waited for Blandine and Yvonne. Soon they arrived, she was dressed and then her hair was styled. Finally they turned her toward her mirror. She looked lovely in her bridal dress.

'You are a beautiful, radiant bride,' they both told her. Then off they walked to the Church of Saint Joan where Jacques, looking handsome in a new suit and shirt, was waiting. The church was filled with well wishers.

'Come my beautiful bride, Clotilde. Everyone awaits us.' He kissed her and pressed an exquisite bouquet of sweetly scented flowers into her hands. Slowly they entered the church, took part in the mass and exchanged their vows. 'With Clotilde at my side I can achieve anything,' Jacques thought to himself. And Clotilde happily mused, 'Jacques, you have given me your love and you have also given me a name. Before today I was only Clotilde, nothing more, but now I am Madame Vallon. '

Tables and benches had been set up under the trees in the Government garden by Clotilde's pupils, where all gathered to toast the bride and groom and enjoy the wedding refreshments. As the shadows lengthened Clotilde and Jacques finally left for their new home, to begin their lives together on this happiest of days.

14

Time passed quickly for Clotilde through the demands of work, teaching and maintaining a home. In late July she experienced strange bouts of sickness in the morning. She could teach without this problem if she missed her breakfast and only in September was Clotilde's first pregnancy fully confirmed. Her sickness passed and she was told a new baby would arrive in March of the following year.

'Jacques, what we had suspected is now certain. I am carrying our first child.'

'What wonderful news! Our first baby will arrive after Christmas. I had always hoped to have a family to care for.'

'I am looking forward to becoming a mother. I love children and now we will have one of our very own.'

Vivienne was also overcome with joy. 'It is so fortunate for us all that this school will close at the end of the year. Are you well enough to carry on with your teaching, Clotilde?

'I will continue to teach until the end of October, but after that I would like to spend the last months of my pregnancy at home. By then I will need more rest and I must take time to prepare a room for the baby. There are so many things to finish in our new home and I could also spend more time in our garden if I wasn't teaching.'

'Clotilde, your wishes will be respected. An early end to the school year will give us a chance to unpack all the supplies here and move them into the new church school. By then the building will be finished and the nuns will have arrived. They also will need time to settle in and prepare for their new teaching year.'

Speaking later to Jacques, all agreed that this was a perfect solution to their situation. 'I won't miss teaching at all if I have a new baby to care for. I also want to continue my work as a botanical artist and help you develop the seed bank.'

The year soon reached its end and Clotilde said a final farewell to her pupils.

In late March of the following year she and Jacques became the proud parents of a beautiful baby girl. During her christening, they named their first little daughter, Celeste. With mother and baby settled at home, Jacques' life continued in many new directions. His hard work in the Government Garden was made much easier by the training he offered to his two apprentices. Their assistance eased his burden. Both were strong, capable young men, eager to work and learn all he could teach them.

Jacques had also begun to catalogue the many varieties of seed plants that grew throughout Nouvelle-Caledonie. He set up contacts as far afield in the island as he could. These field workers brought him plant materials, with their roots intact, on a flowering stem.

'Clotilde, I have five packets of fresh seeds that need your helping hand. Will you wash them in plain water and spread them out in the sun to dry? Be sure to keep them carefully separated from each other. '

'I'll prepare them one at a time so none can be mixed with the others. Shall I label the envelopes for the dry seeds as well?'

'This would be such a help to me as the collection is steadily growing. We won't know their correct botanical name, others will determine this, but I'll provide you with their indigenous plant names for the envelope identification.'

They ran out of storage space so quickly that a large shed had to be built in the far corner of their land. This included an office and many shelves to hold their collection. A long table and several chairs were also needed on the back veranda, where Clotilde could work as the baby slept. A railing was added too, so when Celeste could finally move around, she wouldn't stray into the garden and beyond. Within six months, Jacques had accumulated enough seed packets to send on to France, aboard a departing ship.

'I am also expecting several unusual flowers to arrive from Tahiti. These are plants that grow only on that island. I'm told they are members of the orchid family and are all very beautiful.'

Later Jacques excitedly brought back a sample of several flowers to show Clotilde. 'Here is a temple flower, the Tamanu, a white frangipani. It has a wonderful scent. Just look at this brilliant orange hibiscus and smell the Tiari Tahiti, a rare gardenia. I also particularly like this lovely white lily.'

'What is the orchid called?' Clotilde asked. 'It has glowing white petals with a deep purple lip.'

'You are holding a rare Tahitian vanilla orchid that grows nowhere else in the world.'

'Jacques, place it in water until I can complete a drawing of it. I've never seen anything before quite like this blossom.'

The drawing she finished was one of her best, as she skilfully shaded the white petals with their slight blue tinge and contrasted this with a deep purple lip and labia. 'Insects are drawn to the protruding lip of every orchid where they rest and leave pollen. Without the bees, no orchids would reproduce themselves,' Jacques told her.

'I have an idea,' said Clotilde. 'There are so many different orchids, why don't I make a series of drawings featuring these flowers. It could become our *Florilegium* - a special collection of exotic orchids from Tahiti and Nouvelle-Caledonie. What do you think?'

'Clotilde, this is a wonderful project for us both to undertake! I'll bring you any orchid that reaches me, then you can draw and colour the botanical illustration for each. Be sure to leave a space in the lower left hand corner of each drawing where you will enter the flower's name, location and date in your fine handwriting.' And so the *Florilegium* project was begun.

✳ ✳ ✳

As the years passed the Vallon family grew. Two boys arrived followed by another daughter. In addition to his work as chief gardener of the Government Garden, Jacques continued to receive many new horticultural commissions. By 1875 Noumea had grown into a thriving port and city with over a thousand residents. Some of the former convicts who had received pardons and a piece of land chose to remain on the island. As a steady stream of free settlers also continued to arrive by ship, the Governor and City Council Fathers decided that a Town Hall should now be built. Jacques was commissioned to landscape the surrounds of the attractive white timber building. Flowering shrubs were planted within decorative flower beds around three sides of the Noumea Town Hall. In the large space behind the building, Jacques created an unusual concept in horticulture – that of the perfumed garden - the first of its kind in the South Pacific. Benches were scattered along its two free flowing pathways where the people of Noumea could stroll and inhale the fragrances of heavily scented flowers and herbs.

Clotilde's life too, was a full and busy one, caring for her home and family, assisting Jacques with the seed bank and now teaching the art of botanical illustration to several young women. Her *Florilegium* continued to grow as more and more art works found their place between its leather tooled covers and ever expanding binding. Life for Clotilde, Jacques and their four children was good. Every moment had been a long and joyful adventure.

Of late, fewer letters reached Mater Dei, as the sisters she had known and loved slowly aged and died. Only Mother Germain was left. Now ninety-seven years of age and nearly blind, she required others to read her correspondence aloud to her. In Clotilde's final letter, her happy life filled with stories about her children and Jacques' success, was shared with all. At its end she thanked Mother Germain for offering her the opportunity to sail to Grande Terre those many years ago. But it was Mother Germain, as always, who had the last word.

'Yes, right from the beginning we knew that our Clotilde was a special young woman. We all watched her grow and mature with such grace and ease. It brings me great joy to learn that during these many years, spent away from us at Mater Dei, she has now fulfilled her promise. '

Author's Note

In October 1774 aboard HMS *Resolution*, Captain James Cook sighted a tiny island. It measured eight miles by five miles lying in the Pacific Ocean east-north-east of where the city of Sydney now stands. Cook claimed the island, naming it in honour of the Duchess of Norfolk. Going ashore, he noted the island was uninhabited, had abundant fresh water, good soil, towering spruce pines, plentiful bird life, and fish.

On the following day Cook left 'Paradise,' as he described Norfolk Island, but a paradise it was not destined to be. From 1788 until 1855 England created a brutal prison colony on Norfolk for its worst offenders. Peace returned to the island only after 1856 when the prison closed and the descendants of Fletcher Christian, his fellow mutineers from the famous ship, *Bounty*, and their Tahitian wives arrived from Pitcairn Island.

Also located in the heart of the South Pacific, New Caledonia was named and claimed by Captain Cook. It lies east of Queensland, Australia and northwest of New Zealand. A large archipelago over 500 miles in length, New Caledonia is composed of the mainland, the Isle of Pines, and the Loyalty Islands. With its profusion of native flora and fauna and a richly diverse marine environment, it is one of the most beautiful archipelagos in the world. Initially claimed for England, in 1847 the French Navy - backed up by a military contingent - landed at Balade to secure the island. Colonization began in earnest at Port-de-France in 1855. New Caledonia still remains a French territory today.

Apart from the historical figures and well-known places mentioned in the text, all of the locations and characters in these two stories are fictional.